"Do you have to leave again?"

As she asked the question, Elizabeth looked up at Travis, anguish in her heart.

"I can't stay, really. Maybe if things were different . . . but there's someone in my life," he said as he edged closer to her, "someone I want too much."

"*Someone?*" Elizabeth murmured, struggling against him as she tried to absorb the implication of his words.

"Oh, honey, can't you see? *You're* that someone—you're the only woman in my life, and I don't want to hurt you." As his hands roamed her bare shoulders and his mouth pressed damp kisses along her neck, she relaxed, delighting in each touch of his mouth on her tingling flesh.

"Don't go now, Travis. I want you, too. So much." Her fingers wove through his hair, pressing him even closer.

"Are you sure you're ready for this, Elizabeth? I mean—you just had a baby not so long ago."

"I'm more than ready," she replied huskily, feeling the heat of his body against her.

"Then, sweetheart, show me the way. . . ."

Binnie Syril has created another gripping, emotional tale with her third Temptation title, *Baby Love*. Although she doesn't have any children herself, Binnie has spent many hours watching over her own niece as an infant. Writing about the dilemma of a surrogate mother with no parents to give her child to was no easy feat. And while Binnie was working on *Baby Love*, she often referred to it as "my labor of love." In her usual sensitive way, she explores every facet of a difficult situation—the loneliness, the fear, but also the joyful wonder of caring for a child originally destined for someone else.

Binnie's first Temptation, *The Color of Love*, was a finalist in the Romance Writers of America Golden Medallion contest.

Books by Binnie Syril

HARLEQUIN TEMPTATION
247–THE COLOR OF LOVE
276–OUT OF THE DARKNESS

Baby Love

BINNIE SYRIL

Harlequin Books

TORONTO • NEW YORK • LONDON
AMSTERDAM • PARIS • SYDNEY • HAMBURG
STOCKHOLM • ATHENS • TOKYO • MILAN

To Dominique Mondoulet-Wise—a gem of an editor
who helped to see me through this labor of love

Published June 1991

ISBN 0-373-25452-0

BABY LOVE

1

SILENCE GREETED Travis Logan as he entered his brother and sister-in-law's suburban Baltimore town house. Home is where the heart is. "Was," he corrected himself bleakly as he carried his suitcase inside and shut the front door against the bone-chilling January wind and late-afternoon darkness.

It looked like a house, but to Travis, it was a cold, empty shell that waited in vain for two people who were never coming back. Although it had happened nearly a week ago, he still couldn't believe it, couldn't accept it. Rick and Kathy were dead. They had gone to New York on vacation. On the way back from a concert at Lincoln Center, their cab had been broadsided by a truck. They hadn't had a chance.

Travis gazed unseeingly at the forest of plants that Kathy had cultivated over the years, and at the mockery of a house with nobody in it. He didn't see the bright airiness created by the sheer curtains, nor did his gaze linger on the furniture that had been selected for comfort as well as style. All he was aware of was the dull ache in his head; he couldn't stop remembering. He was to have met them for dinner the next day. Instead, he had received the call from the New York police, informing him of their deaths.

By all rights, Travis should have been at his Connecticut base of operations, straightening out the problems of an automated system he had designed. But because of the brutality of fate, he was hundreds of miles away from there, standing in the living room of the house that Kathy had so painstakingly decorated.

Jamming clenched fists into his pockets, Travis felt a driving need to clear up Rick's and Kathy's affairs, get out, and get back to his Connecticut condo that wasn't a home, either. Heaven knew, he'd rather be anywhere but here. If he never saw this place—this empty house again, it would be too soon. He withdrew his hands from his pockets and wiped them on the sides of his slacks. Then, he picked up his suitcase and made his way into the den.

He set the suitcase down next to the desk, then took off his jacket and dropped it over the back of the chair. He tugged viciously at the knot in his tie, then seated himself at his brother's desk.

"I don't want to do this," he muttered, closing his eyes briefly. Then, taking a deep breath, he flicked on the lamp. He'd have to pretend that this was a logic problem similar to those he faced every day as a computer consultant. Besides, there was really no other family to take care of this. Kathy had had one or two distant cousins who were up in years, and he'd been Rick's only family ever since their mother had died five years earlier.

There was simply no one else to do what had to be done.

A cursory search of the desk turned up three envelopes, one labeled Contract, the other two labeled Wills. He tossed the contract envelope aside, assuming it must relate to Rick's business. The other two envelopes he left on the desk. Rick's and Kathy's wills. At first, he couldn't bring himself to touch them, telling himself that the documents could wait until he spoke with Rick and Kathy's lawyer. But what was the point of waiting? he asked himself. A delay wouldn't change the facts. Gritting his teeth, he read through the wills, plowing through the legal language that named him as beneficiary to their estate. As if he cared about the money, he thought.

About to refold the documents, he noticed that each had the same codicil. He stared in disbelief: a large portion of the estate was to be held in trust for any children. "What children?" he asked, sinking back into the chair. Rick and Kathy had tried for years to have a child, with no success. There'd been miscarriages, fertility clinics, and fruitless attempts at adoption. Finally, it had been tacitly agreed that the subject wouldn't be brought up again. They had died still hoping that someday...

"Ah, hell!"

Forcing himself to calm down, Travis realized that the language about children was just that. Language. There *was* no child. Determinedly, he refolded the wills and directed his attention to the desktop computer he'd given his brother and sister-in-law two years ago.

He didn't really think a search of the computer files would yield anything of substance, but he sifted through the file directory anyway. What he found was typical stuff for a home computer—accounts, recipes. He smiled remembering some of Kathy's culinary concoctions. Then something caught his eye—a file named Baby.

"What the—!" He called the file up on screen, and found himself looking at a list of prospective baby names. And then, to his shock, the next screen was a draft of a birth announcement:

Kathleen and Richard Logan
are
proud to announce
the
birth of their son/daughter on

"Pregnant!" Shaking his head in disbelief he sank back in the chair. Kathy had been pregnant. When had she been due? And what difference did it make now, he reminded himself grimly. Had he, Travis, been so concerned with work and so out of touch that he had missed the fact that Kathy was pregnant? And then it hit him: they hadn't wanted to tell him until they'd had their baby. They'd waited, hoped, prayed for so long. And then to have it all end this way...

There would be no baby to inherit their estate. Kathy was dead, and her unborn child had died with her.

Why that cab? Why them? Why hadn't the driver taken another route? *Why?* he agonized.

He didn't realize he'd been pounding on the desk until the edge of his clenched fist started to ache. He'd never realized that he was capable of displaying so much emotion.

To escape the green-on-black words wavering in front of his burning eyes, he got up, heading for the spare room he'd used on his rare visits to his brother's house. But it was on passing the other guest room that he got a real kick in the guts: it was decorated as a nursery, complete with storybook wallpaper, an intricate wooden mobile, and a white wicker bassinet bordered with a long skirt. Somehow, the empty room made the tragedy all the more real, his own loss ragged and raw. He leaned against the door frame feeling sick. Finally, he turned away and went on to his own room, intending to lie down for a while, even though falling asleep was highly unlikely.

ELIZABETH CHAPMAN was tired and achy, and glad that the driving was over, at least for a while. She had almost postponed the trip. The ever-increasing fatigue of her nearly nine-month pregnancy was sapping her strength.

It was five-thirty, and already it was dark. For the better part of the day, she'd taken the easy way out, putting the finishing touches on several woodworking projects. But finally, a strong sense of commitment had forced her to make the drive to Pikesville. Of course, the plants wouldn't die if their watering schedule was off by a day, she told herself. But it wouldn't be too bright to leave the newspapers on the lawn, and the mail in the box. It would be a dead giveaway to uninvited visitors.

This would be her last trip out to water the plants. Rick and Kathy were due back from New York. They'd wanted to stay close, since they were her delivery room coaches. But she'd assured them she'd be fine. And she was, she exulted, laughing out loud for the sheer joy of it all. But that didn't mean that she wasn't anticipating their return.

As if sharing her excitement, the child she carried under her heart began its now-familiar soft-shoe routine when she eased her way carefully out of her van. "Soon, little one," she murmured, patting the taut roundness of her stomach. "Soon you'll be seeing Mommy and Daddy." As she walked to the front door, she smiled at her fancifulness in talking to the unborn child. "At least there's no one listening in. They'd think I was going bonkers." And then she shook her head with a laughing groan, realizing that she was thinking out loud again.

It wasn't until Elizabeth reached the door that it dawned on her that the newspapers were nowhere to be seen. Strange, but not unheard of. The mailbox was empty, too. There wasn't even any junk mail. Well, there were still the plants to be watered, she told herself as she fumbled with the key to the front door.

She entered the house, shivering a bit at the chill of the unheated interior. One glance around assured her that the place was as empty as it had been for the last week and a half. They weren't home yet. Of course not, she sighed as she took off her down jacket and went to get the watering can. She'd just received the "I ♥ New York" postcard from them that morning.

As she passed the study, a flash of green and black caught her eye. The computer was on; from the doorway, she could see the screen displaying the birth announcement. There was a jacket over the back of the chair and a suitcase on the floor beside the desk. Her heart beat faster. No wonder the papers were missing and the mailbox empty; they'd come home early after all. How dear of them! Plants forgotten, a smile lit her face as she went upstairs, calling out a greeting. "Rick? Kathy?"

THE HAIRS LIFTED on the back of Travis's neck as sounds slid through the house's waiting silence. A door opening and closing. Slow footsteps. His brother's name. Dear God, he muttered. What now? When he'd seen the pile of newspapers and mail on the kitchen table, he'd reckoned a neighbor had been coming in every day. Having to make polite conversation was the last thing Travis felt like doing. Muscles tightened in anticipation as he left his room and went to investigate.

He found what he was looking for in the baby's room: a lady in a faded pink sweat suit. Her back was to him; all he could see was her shapely derriere, and a mane of wildly curly auburn hair. When she turned, he saw at once that she was very pregnant. He felt his heart catch at the sweetness of the smile on her face—and then watched the smile fade as fear took its place.

SHE FOUND HERSELF face-to-face with a stranger.

She took a step backward, then another, until her trembling legs were pressed against the edge of the window frame. There was nowhere else she could go. Even if she hadn't been in an advanced stage of pregnancy, she couldn't have outrun him. Furthermore, she had nothing to protect herself with.

He was tall, perhaps over six feet, well-built. His thick, straight caramel colored hair was tousled, a shock of it flopping over his forehead. Brown-gold eyes behind steel-rimmed glasses seemed to freeze her in place. Her tongue flicked out to moisten parched lips. "Please. Take whatever you want. There isn't much. Just—"

He shook his head, taking a step into the room, but halted immediately as her arms folded protectively across her distended stomach. Her breathing had quickened until she was almost panting, her breasts heaving erratically against the soft fabric of the oversize top she wore. "Don't be afraid. I didn't mean to frighten you."

She said nothing, but something in the sandpaper-rough texture of his voice seemed to take the edge off her rising hysteria.

"I've never hurt a pregnant lady in my life, I promise you."

When she didn't respond to his light attempt at humor, he said, "Look, I guess you must be a friend of Rick's and Kathy's. Well, I'm Travis Logan, and—"

"Travis!" It was going to be all right, she told herself, almost fainting in relief. He was Rick's younger brother. "I can't believe this! According to Kathy, you hardly ever get down here for a visit, and now you've come and they're in New York. I'm Elizabeth Chapman, by the way. I came here to water the plants, and—"

"Ms. Chapman."

She took a deep breath. "I'm sorry. I know I'm chattering. I don't, usually. I—I guess I'm just feeling nervous. I've never discovered an almost-burglar before," she said, laughing weakly, and easing away from the window. Looking as if she had just tumbled out of bed also embarrassed her. She didn't bother asking herself about this uncustomary concern with her looks.

He knew he couldn't let her go ahead and water the plants as if it were business as usual. Neither did he want to say the words that had to be said. But she obviously didn't know what had happened to Rick and Kathy. He came into the room, his gaze momentarily shifting to the empty crib, then back to the woman standing in front of him. "Ms. Chapman, I—I don't exactly know how to say this."

She cocked her head to the side, noticing for the first time how tired and worn-out the man looked. His lean-planed face was dusted with five-o'clock shadow. And now that he'd come closer, she could see that his brown-gold eyes were red-rimmed.

According to Kathy, Travis was eight years younger than Rick, who was nearly forty. But right now, Travis looked as if *he* were the older brother. Kathy had often referred to Travis as a workaholic with a nomadic life-style. Evidently, Travis Logan worked very hard at what he did. "Is something wrong?" she asked softly as she saw his mouth tighten, and his hands clench and unclench at his sides.

"You're not just doing the watering as a neighborly gesture, are you?"

She blinked up at him, wondering at the oddness of the question. "Well, I'm not exactly a neighbor. I live about six miles from here. But I would've come even if I lived farther away than that. Why?"

"Then you and Rick and Kathy were pretty good friends, weren't you?"

"Best friends," she replied unhesitatingly, suffused by a sense of warmth. And then, she stiffened, her mind flashing back to one word, "What do you mean, 'were'?"

"They're not coming back."

"Of course they are!" she snapped, her eyes flashing blue-green fire. "They would have told me if they'd planned to relocate. They said nothing about it. They were even talking about buying a bigger house. You must have been pretty out of touch."

"I think you'd better sit down," he suggested, indicating the nearby rocking chair.

Something in his manner, in the way he was looking at her was making her nervous. After all, what did she really know about this man? And her judgment of men had never been in the range of the superlative, she reminded herself wryly. "Just say what you have to say, Mr. Logan, and then I can do what I came to do and leave."

He took a deep breath, determined to deliver the news in the gentlest way possible. He had to force the words past the lump in his throat. "Rick and Kathy—they were killed in an accident in New York four days ago."

Elizabeth heard the words the man was saying, but every instinct in her fought against their meaning until the world turned black around her.

Travis caught her as she swayed toward him, his large hands grasping the delicate bones of her shoulders. Her head lolled back, exposing her slender throat. With great care, he slid one arm under her knees, gently lifting her into his arms. As he cradled her against his chest, her head seemed to nestle under his chin. She was so warm, and soft, and so very light. She hardly weighed anything, despite the advanced state of her pregnancy.

He brought her to his room and lay her on the bed, reluctant to relinquish his hold on her. Her hair was a red-gold nimbus around her face, her skin almost translucent. She was in shock, he realized as he went to the bathroom to dampen a washcloth.

As SHE REGAINED consciousness, Elizabeth first prayed that the man named Travis Logan and the message he carried were all part of a nightmare. But sensations filtered through: The damp roughness of a cloth being gently smoothed over her face. The warm flesh of a masculine hand brushing the hair back from her clammy forehead. The living weight of him next to her on the bed.

Forcing her eyes open, she looked up into the face of nightmare—and saw reality. The man was real, and the awful words he'd spoken could not be taken back. "N-not both," she begged, feeling the hot tears overflow at the grim set of his mouth and the curt nod of his head.

For long moments she drifted in a kind of limbo, tears trickling into her hairline. Then, an agonizing shaft of physical pain underscored her grief. She closed her eyes, biting her lips, praying for control. It was just a false contraction; she'd had them before. It would pass. It would have to.

"What's wrong?" Travis asked, seeing the sweat break out on her forehead.

She shook her head. "N-nothing," she gasped, sighing in relief as the pain subsided. "I'll be fine."

She didn't *look* fine, but he said nothing about that. "Is it— are you in labor?"

"It's not the real thing. I've had these false alarms before. I've got to get home."

"Rest awhile. Then I'll drive you." He reached for the damp washcloth once more, not knowing if it was doing any good, but knowing that doing something—anything—had to be better than nothing. And all the while, he wondered at the odd way her pain had lanced through him.

Taking his advice she lay back, thinking about the feel of him next to her, the cloth he soothed over her face like a caress. "No," she moaned softly, shivering as a warm trickle dampened her thighs. Her body had been acutely sensitive throughout her pregnancy. Now she lay there in disbelief.

"What is it?" he asked.

She bit her lip. "Nothing," she managed. Her water breaking. . . . It *can't* be happening now, she pleaded silently. The one thought at the forefront of her mind was getting home. But first, she had to get up, she realized, mentally bracing herself for the effort. The slight dampness between her legs was uncomfortable, not to mention embarrassing.

"You should rest a while longer," he said, automatically easing her down to the bed as she struggled to sit up.

She shook her head. "I'll—be fine. My van's outside."

"You shouldn't be alone."

"I'll—I'll manage."

And then all thought was wiped out as another red-hot spasm wrenched at her insides.

Terror seized Travis at her taut, jerky movements next to him on the bed. Her face contorted in a rictus of agony. "Elizabeth, is it the baby?"

"Too—too early," she gasped. "It can't come now. It—" she broke off, trying to conserve her strength, trying somehow to figure out how many minutes had elapsed between the first pain and the second.

"Tell me what to do," he said, clasping her hand gently in his own.

She tried to remember everything she and Rick and Kathy had rehearsed. "Count—the minutes—between pains."

One eye on Elizabeth, one eye on his watch, Travis hoped against hope that her pains were over. He had the unfamiliar sensation of being out of control, of being unable to master the terror that coursed through him at the thought of the helpless woman beside him. He dreaded her pain as if it were his own and felt echoes of it in his own body when six minutes later, a spasm threatened to tear her apart.

She was grasping his hand as if it were a lifeline, barely aware that he made no protest when her nails scored his flesh.

There was so little he could do for her. "I've got to get you some help. Who can I call?"

"My doctor. Doctor Alan Goldstein," she panted, reeling off her obstetrician's number. "I hope he's there."

"If he's not, they'll find him," Travis said in what he hoped were reassuring tones. "You just lie still, try to relax," he urged, squeezing her hand gently before reaching for the phone. He got an answering service, and was immediately told to bring Elizabeth to Garland Memorial's emergency room entrance. The doctor would meet them at the hospital.

Travis glanced down at Elizabeth, who was looking up at him, her eyes glazed with pain. He gritted his teeth, frustrated because he was unable to do anything to reduce her suffering. He didn't question the inordinate concern he had for a woman he didn't even know. He just knew that more than anything else, he wanted to take her into his arms and tell her everything would be all right. He looked into her eyes once more, and beyond her pain he also saw profound sadness.

He shifted on the bed.

"Don't go," she gasped.

"I've got to get you ready to go to the hospital. I'll be careful, don't worry," he said as he got a blanket from the end of the bed and carefully wrapped it around her.

"I—I know you'll be careful," she said, trying to ignore the fact that, no matter what, everything hurt, from her eyelashes down to her toenails. But he looked and sounded so sincere. "I know you will."

THE DRIVE THROUGH the cold of the January evening seemed to take forever. The road was unfamiliar; he had to ask Elizabeth for directions. And to Travis's frustration, all he could do was touch her hand every once in a while, wincing at each groan that came through her lips, each twist of her body in its fruitless attempts to escape the pain. It was as if he were connected to her somehow, each stab of pain she felt echoing in his own body. The feeling left him dazed; this had never happened to him before. And each touch they shared, no matter how slight, seemed to reinforce an almost electrical connection—as if he were using an improperly grounded computer keyboard in a thunderstorm.

He risked a sideways glance at her. She didn't look like a storm goddess. Her eyes were closed, her small fists buried in the fleece-lined upholstery. Her head shifted from side to side, as if she were trying to dodge the pain. Never had he known such fear, felt so responsible for another person's life. For two lives, he amended silently. His hand tensed on the gearshift, as he instinctively pushed the car faster than the legal limit.

"Soon, honey. We'll be there soon," he ground out, not even wondering at the endearment that slipped out unnoticed by either one of them. He felt a sharp stab of pain across his middle. Logic told him it was the result of too little food and too little rest. He was ripe for an ulcer if he didn't slow down and take better care of himself, his doctor had warned him months before. But the biggest part of the pain came from his heart, where the grief over Rick's and Kathy's deaths lodged like a canker. And from the thought of the travail Elizabeth was enduring.

"Is there anyone you want me to call? Your husband?"

She shook her head vehemently. "I'm not married," she bit out, not wanting to be reminded, even in passing, of Dennis Chapman, the man who had once been her husband.

"Is there anyone you want—there for you? Family?"

Not now, not anymore. Who could she call? Elizabeth mocked inwardly. "My father's dead. There's only my mother. She lives in Arizona. And we're not close. I guess you could say she doesn't approve of my—pregnancy."

He barely managed to avoid cursing under his breath. "Friends, then."

Who else was there now that Rick and Kathy were gone? Her throat clogged with despair. "There's Jenny Fairhall. I work with her husband Brad. But I'm not as close with them as I was with Rick and Kathy. I haven't known Jenny and Brad as long."

"Never mind that. What's Jenny's number?"

"Don't bother," Elizabeth sighed, tensing in her seat as the car rounded a curve. "Brad's teaching a class tonight and Jenny's stranded with three kids. There's nothing either of them could do but worry." And more than that, she was forced to admit to herself, calling would mean explanations. And with her feelings scraped raw and bleeding, she could barely function. She couldn't cope with anything else right now.

And then she was forced to swallow the sobs that threatened to overwhelm her, knowing that the only two people she wanted more than anyone else in the world—the people who had truly breached the walls of her carefully constructed independence—would be there only in her heart. "Th-there's no one for you to call."

To his amazement, he felt the tightness in his chest slacken at Elizabeth's response. What about the man in her life? Travis found himself wondering. What about the man responsible for the pain and suffering she was going through? One thing was certain: that man wasn't concerned enough to be there with her. Was she widowed, divorced, coming off a broken relationship?

Wouldn't she want the father to know? Deeply affected by Elizabeth's aloneness, Travis shook his head. It shouldn't be that way. If it were *his* child, no matter what the circumstances, he would certainly want to know. And to be at her side . . .

When they reached the hospital, Travis parked near the emergency room entrance and carried Elizabeth inside. An attendant materialized with a wheelchair.

As Travis lowered her into the wheelchair, she looked up at him, extending her right hand. "Thank you for all you've done."

He shook his head, taking her cold hand in both his warm ones. "Thanks is the last thing I want," he said. Without hesitating, he asked, "Do you mind if I stay and wait, then? Unless you've changed your mind about my contacting one of your friends."

"You don't have to stay," she whispered, her voice rusty with suppressed tears.

She'd ignored the last part of his question, he noticed, recalling all too well her reaction to Rick's and Kathy's deaths. She was swamped by grief, and all alone at a time like this. Even now her mouth was trembling. Somehow, he was sure that his brother and sister-in-law would have wanted him to stay with Elizabeth. He hunkered down in front of the wheelchair, so she wouldn't have to crane her neck to look up at him. Her eyes were red, filmed with exhaustion and pain. "I want to stay."

"It might take a long time, Travis."

"I don't care how long it takes," he said. And was rewarded by her tremulous smile. The smile was immediately transformed into a grimace as pain shot through her.

"Are you sure I can't contact anyone for you, Elizabeth?"

She couldn't stem the flow of tears that welled up, drenching her lashes, flooding her cheeks. "Rick and Kathy. They were my best friends."

There was no way to phrase the next question delicately; Travis had been skirting it ever since he'd laid eyes on Elizabeth. "What about the baby's father?" he asked, his heart contracting as he saw her eyes fill with tears once more. Could it be that the man involved hadn't wanted a child? Or maybe it was simply that she felt her biological clock running down, and she wanted to experience motherhood.

"Time for Ms. Chapman to visit the examination room," a woman in white informed them.

"Wait," Elizabeth pleaded with the nurse. Travis would have to know sometime, Elizabeth thought with trepidation, and somehow, she knew the time would have to be now, in case anything happened. "Rick—Rick's the father."

2

"WHAT!"

"Travis—"

And then there were no more words, as Elizabeth was wheeled away by the nurse, and Travis was left staring in shock.

Too stunned to do more than remain rooted to the terrazzo floor in the emergency room, Travis was startled to hear someone call his name. It was the nurse who had been with Elizabeth moments before.

"We've taken her up to the birthing center. Ms. Chapman's given permission for you to wait up there and be informed about the baby's birth."

"Permission?"

"If your name's not on the approved list, you can't go to the waiting lounge. You wouldn't even get as far as the elevator. Security. You have to register with them before you go up."

Travis got a pass from the security guard and went upstairs, not bothering to tell the nurse that *nothing* could have made him leave.

As he stepped off the elevator on the sixth floor, rage simmered inside him. "I can't believe it," he muttered, incredulous at Elizabeth's attempt to foist her child's paternity on someone who couldn't dispute it. Without a doubt, the woman had her eye on the main chance. But then he remembered her agony—the tragedy of turquoise eyes that were kaleidoscopes of fear and grief and other emotions he couldn't name. And Travis knew that whatever else the woman was, whatever sins she might be guilty of, lying about the father of her child wasn't one of them. Clearly, Elizabeth had cared about the father of her child.

Despite the facts that hammered at him all too clearly, Travis still couldn't believe the evidence that had come from the woman's own mouth. It was too incongruous. She simply didn't look the part. And he never would have believed that Rick was capable of betraying Kathy. Wishing he still smoked, he paced, trying to find solace, as he usually did, in logic. Instead, his circuits jammed as he tried to reconstruct the death of his brother's perfect marriage.

He'd thought Elizabeth had been abandoned by the father of her child. Now he knew that his own brother had been responsible. Travis's mind gravitated to the only possible logical conclusion: Rick was the father of Elizabeth Chapman's child. Elizabeth Chapman was—had been—his brother's lover.

Then why was he, Travis, so reluctant to accept what was so obviously the truth? Because none of it made any sense. According to Elizabeth, Rick and Kathy were her best friends. Her shock—her complete emotional breakdown—hadn't seemed faked. But what kind of "best friend" goes to bed with her "best friend's" husband? Travis asked himself in bewilderment.

Sitting in the deserted lounge, he sipped vile black coffee from a plastic cup in an effort to energize a tired mind that was suffering from emotional overload. Finally, he wound down, settling back onto a vinyl sofa as he waited with tensely suppressed impatience for his brother's child to be born. With a little effort, he could almost imagine that Elizabeth was just a part of the nightmare that was Rick's death. Beyond that, he couldn't think. He tried not to think at all....

Travis stared down at his fists, seeing the remnants of half-moon-shaped indentations that still scored the backs of his hands. He winced as he recalled how Elizabeth had anchored herself to his flesh when the pain had racked her body. Even now, in the hushed quiet of the hospital, he couldn't forget her cries, or the way her hands had latched onto his as if he were her anchor in a storm-tossed world. He stared down at his hands again, his vision blurring. It was almost as if he were branded, and linked to her by an invisible chain.

SURROUNDED BY a hospital staff that went about their duties like a well-oiled machine, Elizabeth had no concept of the passage of time. She was attached to a fetal monitor, regowned, poked, prodded and "ah-hahed" over, until she was sure that the tearing pain inside her would be a permanent condition. Certainly, it showed no signs of letting up.

"I don't—suppose—this is false labor?" she asked her doctor—Dr. Goldstein—between short puffs of breath.

"'Fraid not. The good news is that the baby's going to be born sooner rather than later. Where are those two coaches that are supposed to be in the room with you? I thought Rick and Kathy would be here."

"It's—it's just me," she said, her voice breaking as she told him what had happened to her best friends. Through blurred vision, she saw him shake his head sadly. Then she felt a tear slide down her cheek as he took one of her icy hands and held it between his own warm hands.

"It's okay, Elizabeth. I know you've had a terrible shock, but trust me. We have everything you'll need. We'll help you."

"But after—the baby—"

"Don't worry about anything now. Let's take one step at a time. For now, the first step is birth. The nurses are ready and waiting to stand in as coaches. We'll get you through this."

As labor continued, Elizabeth's mind wandered, thinking of all the plans they'd made—Rick with a video camera to film the birth, Kathy with a stopwatch to time the contractions. For the first time in years, Elizabeth recalled sadly, she would have been part of a family unit. She'd have helped her friends realize their dearest wish—and her own. Now, that dream was shattered forever as Elizabeth looked up at the faces around her and saw only strangers.

She remembered the shock on Travis Logan's face, realizing it must have mirrored the look on her own face when he'd told her that Rick and Kathy were dead. If only there had been time to tell him the rest before the nurse had taken her upstairs. If only she'd known how...

ELIZABETH WAS TIRED of hearing people around her say, "do this, do that," and most of all, "not yet." She wanted water; they wiped her lips with a damp washcloth. She wanted to push against the pain that was clawing at her insides; they told her it wasn't time. She wanted it to be over, wished it were happening to someone else. Focus on something else, they told her.

Focus. Concentrating on an inanimate object was something she'd practiced with Rick and Kathy. They'd practiced using Kathy's crystal paperweight. She bit down on her lip at the memory, casting around frantically for a substitute. But instead of fixing on an inanimate object, her mind zeroed in on a human image; she deliberately concentrated all her thoughts on the man who had said he'd wait for her.

She knew he was there, could picture him. Tall, lean, and strong. She had felt that tempered strength in him from the first time he'd held her in his arms to comfort her, back at the house. And so very gentle, though his voice had often been harsh with anxiety for her. Finding herself on the receiving end of masculine tenderness very nearly overwhelmed her. "Travis," she panted, his name almost a litany in her mind. "Travis." He was all she had to hold onto.

Elizabeth was so convinced that labor was going to last forever that when they started telling her to push, she was surprised, more than anything....

FINALLY, IT WAS OVER. An absence of something. A vacuum,
like dead silence after an explosion. The acute physical pain
had dramatically lessened. And then she heard the sharp,
strong cry of a baby...

"Here's your son," Dr. Goldstein told her, laying the infant on her stomach. "He's perfect, Elizabeth. We did the ini-
tial ten-point test, and everything's fine."

"I'm—glad," she breathed, blurred eyes directed toward
the child she had just borne.

"Do you want to see him—hold him?" the doctor asked.

Her whole body seemed to be shaking from the effort it
took to keep her arms at her sides. "No. Not now."

There was an awkward pause.

"Maybe later," she murmured. "I'm tired now."

"No problem," the doctor replied. "We'll just clean him up
and pop him in the nursery. And we'll take care of you, too,
lady. You deserve a good rest."

"Can't do anything else. Too tired." And she hurt—inside
and out. Pulsating pain traveled through her limbs and reverberated in her head.

She was very tired and had never felt lower. All she wanted
was to escape into the oblivion of sleep. Only one thing held
her back: she couldn't forget the look on Travis Logan's face
when she'd told him of the baby's parentage. She knew she
had to talk to him, get it over with. Once she was back in her
room, she asked the nurse to see if Travis was still in the
waiting area.

"The hunk?" the nurse wanted to know.

Travis's image flashed before Elizabeth's eyes. "I hadn't
noticed." And realized that her words were a lie.

"Well, *I* did," the nurse said. "If he were mine, I'd put a tag
on him so he wouldn't get lost!"

"MR. LOGAN."

Travis looked down, and discovered that what had once

been an empty Styrofoam cup was now a pile of confetti in his lap. He stood up as a nurse approached him, the white scraps of his cup falling unnoticed to the floor. He saw the woman look down at the chart in her hand, then look up, smiling brightly at him. "It's a boy."

"How's Ms. Chapman?"

"She's fine, out of the recovery room and settled in her room. Do you want to see the baby?"

"Yes. And can I see Ms. Chapman?"

"I'll take you," the nurse offered.

He followed the nurse through the maze of hospital corridors, oblivious to personnel weaving in and out of rooms as they carried out their duties. When they reached the nursery with its glassed-in walls, the nurse asked him to wait while she went inside. As he watched, she retrieved a tiny bundle and walked up to the glass.

Travis gazed through the glass wall, setting his jaw as he fought to swallow tears and focus on the infant. This child—this tiny bit of humanity—was his brother's son. No matter what. *His brother's son.* His heart turned over as he swiped at the tears that fogged his glasses and blurred his vision: his family wasn't dead after all. Even though the child had been created outside his brother's marriage, Rick had left him a precious legacy....

"You can come back later, if you like," the nurse informed him as she left the nursery.

Clearing his throat, he repositioned his glasses. "Yeah. Later." He followed her at a deliberately slower pace as he tried to extinguish the fires of his temper, with no idea what he was going to say to Elizabeth Chapman. He knew damned well that he wasn't going to give voice to the inner confusion that splintered his usually well-ordered mind.

His troubled thoughts counterpointed sharply with the sound of his shoes as he followed the nurse down the hall. He was still unable to reconcile himself to the fact that Elizabeth

Chapman had been his brother's lover. Marshaling all his willpower, he was determined to control himself and his emotions.

"Don't stay too long," the nurse warned softly, pausing at the door to a room that was midway down the hall. "She's only been out of recovery for a short while. And there's another lady in there, too. Both new mamas need their sleep."

He entered the semiprivate room, automatically noting that one half of it was filled with flowers and balloons. The other side—Elizabeth's—was bare of everything.

When he saw the fragile-looking figure of Elizabeth who lay shivering in the hospital room, something inside him changed. The white-hot flame of his temper flickered and died.

Except for the cloud of auburn hair that had been pulled back from her face, she seemed almost to fade into the whiteness of the sheets; she seemed more shadow than substance, more imagined than real. He saw her stir, her head move on the pillow. Her eyes were closed, but a silvery streak of tears stained her cheeks. And every once in a while, a shudder passed through her.

He himself was shaken to the core. She turned her head, opening her eyes as he quietly called her name. She looked exhausted. No, more than that, he realized as he read the signs of stress in her face. Ravaged. Her eyes were enormous. Her face, innocent of makeup, was as white as the pillow that cushioned her head. He saw none of the joy that he would have expected from a new mother; what he saw was nothing like images on television or pictures in a magazine. How could she experience joy? The father of her child was dead.

Travis felt the last remnants of anger leech out, to be replaced both by rigidly imposed control and other feelings that were too unfamiliar to name. He felt the hurt in his heart. The questions he'd wanted to ask faded.

"How do you feel, Elizabeth?"

Her eyes widened as he loomed over her. He wasn't the same man who'd held her in his arms several hours before. She remembered how he'd looked when he'd brought her to the hospital. Now, the clean outlines of his face were blurred with the morning roughness of his beard, and his clothes were rumpled as a result of his spending all those hours in a hospital waiting room. But more than that, his mouth was hard, compressed, his eyes cold. She almost wished she hadn't asked the nurse to call him—but he had a right to know. And Elizabeth had an overpowering need to tell him.

Her first answer was wordless, a shrug; even that slight movement hurt. She looked up at him again, fighting for composure as she braced herself for what was to come. "All right. I feel all right." It was a lie.

He could see that it was a lie. "Now can I have the real answer?"

She sighed resignedly. "Cold. Shivery. Shaky. I can't seem to relax. They say it's natural." What she could have added was scared, confused, afraid to think about tomorrow, let alone the future. "It's all right. I'll get another blanket from the nurse later."

Cold. She was cold. "I'll be right back."

"Where are you going?" she asked, startled to see him walking toward the door.

"I'll be back," was all he said in reply.

To her amazement, he headed out of the room. She was inexpressibly touched when he returned moments later with two white blankets, and, then, with endearingly awkward movements, tucked them around her. With that action, he had become once more the man she remembered. Kind and gentle in a totally masculine way. How long would that last when she finally said what she had to say? "Thank you," she murmured softly.

"No problem. Have you seen the baby?"

"Not since—" She swallowed, unable to meet his eyes, her arms still hurting from not holding her child. "I thought he'd be better off in the nursery. Have you—seen him?"

"Yes. He's beautiful. Rick would have been proud."

"They *both* would have been proud," she said, her breath catching in a sob as she choked out the words.

"*Both?*" he echoed.

"Rick and Kathy."

Travis felt as if he were stranded in a boat on the high seas, with no life jacket. "Kathy—*knew?*"

And then Elizabeth understood the reason for his odd look. She'd said Rick was the father; there hadn't been time to tell Travis anything else. And now she was so very tired. "It isn't what you think," she told him in a voice thick with tears.

"What do you mean?"

She read the unasked questions in his eyes and knew that she owed him answers, no matter how painful they were going to be. "What I said to you before—that Rick was the baby's father—"

"I'm not here to judge—" Travis began gruffly, suddenly swamped with feelings he was almost afraid to identify. He tried to tell himself that what he felt was anger at Rick's betrayal of Kathy. But honesty forced him to admit slashing pangs of...he took a deep breath, raking a hand through his hair. Dammit, he was jealous! Of his own brother. With a massive effort, he ground out, "I'm not making any judgments about the way my brother chose to live his life."

Flinching at the harshness of his tone, she blurted out. "I wasn't Rick's lover. I didn't sleep with your brother."

He stared at her.

"Rick and Kathy were the baby's parents. I'm—" She took a deep, shaking breath. "I was a surrogate mother."

His eyebrows shot up as her unbelievable words reverberated endlessly in his brain. At first, his mind was blank. Then images started surfacing—images of news headlines, lawsuits, history-making trials, television talk shows. *Would the shocks never end?* Travis wondered as he sank into the chair at her bedside. He concentrated on keeping a very tight rein on himself. "You were a surrogate mother?" he asked in disbelief.

"Yes. Travis—" Her heart sank as she saw the wheels turning in his head—the unasked questions—the accusations in his eyes. The assumptions he was obviously making carved his face into harsh lines. "Let me explain."

"We're beyond that."

Once more Travis was judging her, as when he'd assumed she'd been Rick's lover. "Please. You don't understand—" Elizabeth was swamped with exhaustion, grief, and hurt at Travis's reaction. She desperately wanted, *needed* to tell him the truth—all of it. But she also had an overwhelming urge to yield to the gray cloud of sleep pressing down on her, stifling her, slowing her thoughts.

He saw the trembling of her mouth, heard the strain in her voice, and knew that she was close to the edge. Too damned close. And his pressuring her for answers had helped put her there. He wanted answers, wanted them badly. But he didn't mind waiting a few hours.

"I'll be back to see you later, Elizabeth."

He was leaving. Her last tangible link with Rick and Kathy was dissolving as he was leaving her alone in the dark chasm of her own thoughts, abandoning her to this world of pain and fear. "Don't go," she pleaded softly, a breathless catch in her voice.

He had to strain to hear her words. "You need to get some rest. Sleep well," he told her. There was no response. Her eyes were closed; she was very nearly asleep.

She heard his footsteps echo, then fade, as he walked out the door—walking out of her life as if he'd never been. She tried to forget the strained look in his eyes. Instead, as the velvet cloud of fatigue enveloped her, she remembered his touch as he had seen to her comfort and guarded her against the cold.

Burrowing under the now triple layer of blankets he'd tucked around her, Elizabeth wished that he hadn't left without hearing the whole story. Everything. As she dug deep for inner resources that up to now she had never tapped, she didn't dare admit, even to herself, that she wished he hadn't left at all. . . .

IN A DAZE, Travis left Elizabeth's room. But even though his mind was focused on her parting words, the gnawing of his stomach forcibly reminded him that he hadn't eaten in more hours than he cared to remember. The choices were limited: eat out or fix something back at the house. He chose a diner on the way home from the hospital. That way, he wouldn't have to bother fixing food himself. He suppressed a shudder at the thought of rattling around in the emptiness he knew would be waiting for him at his brother's house.

As he worked his way through what passed for bacon and eggs and drank yet another cup of coffee, he tried to sort out parts of the puzzle that were niggling at the back of his tired mind: Elizabeth Chapman as surrogate mother. The idea of her as Rick's lover had been a shock; the reality of her as a surrogate mother was a bombshell.

Why hadn't she told him right away, when they'd first met? Then he answered his own question. Had he expected her to come right out and say, "Oh, by the way, I'm a surrogate mother for your brother and sister-in-law"? And when should she have said it, anyway? When he'd surprised her in the house, when she was in labor, or during the actual birth?

And then, as he walked out of the restaurant into the crisp, cold brightness of the new day, he took his thoughts a step further. Why had Rick and Kathy chosen *this* woman to be a surrogate? *What kind of woman was she?* And why had Elizabeth become a surrogate at all? "Monetary rewards," he muttered in cynical response to his own question. She was probably receiving megabucks, thousands, getting well paid for her time. That's what surrogacy was all about, if the headlines about court cases were any measure of the truth.

When he finally got back to the house, he stripped and showered, hoping that the pulsating jets of hot water would relieve the strain and tension of the past five days. Then he wrapped a towel around his waist and poured himself a glass of Jack Daniel's, neat. He paused in the act of lifting it to his lips. He wasn't one to drink in the middle of the day, let alone before noon. But what the hell—his time clock was off, his emotions in turmoil.

Taking the whiskey back to the bedroom with him, he swirled the liquid around in the glass before taking a healthy swallow. Setting the glass on the night table, he stared down at the quilted satin comforter, which still bore the faint imprint of Elizabeth Chapman's body. With a swipe of his hand, he swept back both comforter and sheet. Then he stripped off his towel and lay down naked, staring vacantly at the ceiling.

One shock had followed another, like earthquake aftershocks. How many more were around the corner? What would be next? he wondered bleakly.

"Dammit, Rick. Why didn't you talk to me, tell me what was happening?" And then Travis shook his head in disgust. "When was I ever home? What should Rick have done, left a message with my answering service, or on the computer bulletin board? Terrific idea, Logan."

He brooded, his mind struggling to sort its way through a maze of too many questions—and almost no answers. What he would do about the baby, Travis had no idea. But when faced with a problem, his usual practice was to do something, take positive action.

Only the week before last, the most important thing on his agenda had been a project in Wisconsin, and then another in

Cambridge soon afterward. And now . . . something had begun to grow inside him, something warm thawing the cold numbness of his heart. He felt renewed; Rick's child was alive.

First and foremost, Travis realized, it would now be his responsibility to execute the will, and provide for that child—the child he had yet to hold. A trust fund would have to be established. The baby wouldn't want for anything, Travis decided, his mind racing ahead as he tentatively planned the child's care and education. His taking responsibility is what Rick and Kathy would have wanted, he told himself.

Travis had never had to undertake responsibility for another human life; certainly, he wasn't prepared for it. But family took care of family, no matter what. That was the way he'd been brought up. And he was sure his brother would have wanted it that way.

At the same time, he was all too aware that he would have to play it carefully; Elizabeth had been through a rough time. He grimaced at the memory of her hospital room. The other side had been bright with balloons and flowers; and her half had been so damned bare . . .

He stared at the ceiling as if it were a mirror and he didn't recognize himself. Days of living on a minimum of food, hardly any sleep, and an overabundance of overcharged emotions and stress had sapped his energy. Yielding to the pull of crushing fatigue, he closed his eyes against the light of day.

3

ELIZABETH DRIFTED, hovering between the blackness of oblivion and the faint awareness of her unfamiliar surroundings. She could barely perceive phantom images of a man and woman and a child—images that seemed so real that she had only to reach out and touch them to bring them close. A family. Rick and Kathy—and their son.

Like waves on the shore, the man and woman disappeared, their receding images replaced by the plaintive cry of a child. And for Elizabeth, whose arms ached with emptiness, there was only the terror of the unknown—of trying to walk in footsteps she couldn't fill . . .

The weight of a hand on her shoulder summoned one more image—of the man who had abandoned her the night before. The man who had said he would come back. "Travis," she murmured.

"Ms. Chapman."

Elizabeth fought her way to awareness. The hand on her shoulder belonged to a woman, not a man—a woman in white.

"I'm Paula Davis, one of the day nurses for this part of the maternity wing. Time to get up, Ms. Chapman. How do you feel?"

"Everything hurts—some parts more than others. My breasts—"

"Will you be nursing?"

"No," Elizabeth replied sharply, hoping that the nurse wouldn't ask her to explain.

Stopping lactation could be taken care of with tablets, Elizabeth was told. Walking would help build her strength back up. And she would have to start doing Kegel exercises, which she recalled learning about during prenatal classes. She was also told that a shower and some soaks would ease the soreness from stitches and stretched out muscles.

"A shower sounds great," Elizabeth said with a sigh. With the help of the nurse, Elizabeth very gingerly got out of bed and stuck her feet into paper hospital-issue slippers. "I had no idea I would feel this way," she muttered under her breath as she slowly made her way into the bathroom. "I feel so—drained."

"You will for a while," the nurse said, her hand cupping Elizabeth's elbow.

Elizabeth was congratulating herself on her efforts until she reached the sink and looked up into the mirror above it.

"Oh...my God," she groaned, at the image facing her. Her wan face looked about as interesting as day-old oatmeal. Her eyes were more red than green, and her hair closely resembled an unmanageable thatch. And Travis Logan had seen her like that. "I look like a twenty-nine year old combination of 'Raggedy Anne' and 'L'il Orphan Annie.' I had a suitcase all packed, but I wasn't at home when I went into labor. I don't have anything with me, not even a comb."

"No problem," the nurse assured her. "You take your shower and wash your hair, if you like, and I'll come back with some of the bare essentials."

"Terrific."

Elizabeth showered slowly and carefully. The warm water did wonders to ease some of her aches and pains. By the time she'd stepped out of the shower, the nurse was back with a bag that contained a wide-toothed comb, toothbrush, and other necessities. There was even a tube of lip gloss.

After Elizabeth had made the most of the contents of the bag and tried to tame the snarls in her freshly washed hair, she slowly went back into the room. To her dismay, a meal tray had been wheeled to the bedside table. She wasn't really hungry, she told herself as she lifted the tray cover and gazed at the unappetizing display of orange juice, congealed scrambled eggs and limp toast.

Elizabeth picked up the container of juice and took a long sip. Then, barely concealing a shudder, she picked up the fork and tried the eggs. Surprisingly, they weren't as bad as they looked. But what little appetite she'd managed to conjure up suddenly vanished when the nurse came back to ask if Elizabeth wanted the baby to "room in."

"I hadn't planned on it," Elizabeth said without hesitation. That was true enough. Rick and Kathy were to have had full care of the baby from the outset. They'd all decided it would be better for parental bonding.

"No problem," the nurse said. "More rest for mama that way. Walking to the nursery can be one of your exercises."

Elizabeth took a shuddering breath. "I'll—see how I feel."

"Look, I know you're tired, but you need to be up on your feet and getting your exercise. The nurse's station is just about halfway down the hall from your room. Why don't you try walking down there? Then we can show you the way to the nursery."

"Fine. I'll just—rest awhile after I finish eating and then I'll start my walkathon." When the other woman had left the room, Elizabeth forced herself to make further inroads into the food, eventually managing to choke most of it down. After all, she didn't want to keel over. Pushing the tray table aside, she tried to court sleep for a while, but the constant procession of people into the other half of the room made that impossible. And even if there had been absolute silence, she admitted to herself reluctantly, the clamor of her own thoughts would have made sleep hopeless.

Exercise, the nurse had said. Cautiously, she eased out of the bed and made her way down the hall, grateful for the support afforded her by the thick horizontal wooden bar that ran along the wall. Not caring about direction, she walked aimlessly past the nurse's station, a bank of elevators, and a solarium. Eventually, she rounded a corner. And saw the large sign posted above a wide glass door: NURSERY. She came to a dead stop, knowing that she had gone far enough. Perhaps too far ...

A surge of weakness made her knees buckle; she was grateful for the cool solidity of the wall against her cheek, the solid wooden bar against her damp palms. It was only by focusing all her effort that she managed to get back to her room without collapsing. When she took her next walk, she vowed, she would go in the opposite direction.

Tiredness, she told herself as she once more climbed into the bed and closed her eyes. She catnapped between visits from nurses, only coming fully awake when she heard yet another set of footsteps, and looked up to find her doctor pulling up a chair next to the bed.

"Your stitches look fine so far, but I don't want you to put any strain on them, so no heavy housework, no pushing a vacuum around, and limit your trips up and down the stairs to one or two a day for the first week. No driving for two weeks. Everything else seems okay. We'll let you go home the day after tomorrow."

"Why not tomorrow? I'd really rather be at home," she said with a sigh. *Alone*, she added silently.

"You're tired and stressed," Dr. Goldstein was saying. "Enjoy the rest while you can. You'll make up for it with plenty of sleepless nights later on. Oh, by the way, do you want to use the pediatrician Rick and Kathy picked out, or would you prefer to find one of your own? I can recommend a couple of people."

"I won't need a pediatrician."

"Why not, Elizabeth?"

She shook her head, her throat too full for a reply as she recalled the sign with the word *nursery*. She swallowed hard. "I'm not keeping the baby. I haven't even seen him, and I don't intend to."

Neither the woman on the bed, nor the doctor noticed the man standing mesmerized in the open doorway.

TRAVIS HAD ARRIVED at Elizabeth's room late that afternoon, his arms laden with flowers. The door was partially open, and he could hear her talking to a man. Out of politeness, he started to walk away. But then he stopped dead in his tracks as he overheard bits of the conversation—evidence that his family was disintegrating for a second time . . .

"Have you thought about what you want to do?" Dr. Goldstein was asking.

"I've been thinking about nothing else, Dr. Goldstein. All night. All day. I don't think I'm meant to be a mother. It's not my destiny. There's so much responsibility. I'm scared."

"Many parents feel the same way," the doctor said.

"I'm not a parent. I'm—I *was* a baby hotel."

"Not anymore."

"I don't know what to do."

"There are several options, Elizabeth," Travis heard the doctor say. "You could keep the baby yourself."

"Or—"

"You could put the child up for adoption."

"I suppose that would be the easy way out. Then he would have two loving parents. A normal, loving family would be the best thing for him."

"Elizabeth, your life has been shattered by a major tragedy. Give yourself some time to recover emotionally. You might feel differently once you're less achy and exhausted. If you do decide on adoption, let me know, and I'll have the hospital social worker come in to talk to you. That's a requirement."

"HELL," Travis muttered, bracing himself against the door: *she doesn't even want the baby*. Until now, he hadn't even considered what would happen to the baby. He'd assumed that the child would stay with Elizabeth Chapman. Now he knew that his assumption was way off base. What kind of a mother would give away her own child, he asked himself bitterly.

Obviously, her job was over, Travis thought as he ground his teeth in frustration. She wanted no part of the baby. According to the words of the doctor, she could give it away to whoever wanted it. She could probably even sell the child; people like Rick and Kathy were desperate for babies.

Travis felt as if he'd been poleaxed. He'd had no idea that Elizabeth wouldn't keep the child. He'd even wondered if she would allow him contact with the child; now it appeared that *she* wanted no contact with the infant. His hazy plans of the night before dissipated like fog burned off by a harsh desert sun. His skin felt icy. But at the center of his being was a molten volcanic core of rage at the unfairness of it all.

He had to restrain himself as he heard her say that she wanted the baby to have a normal, loving family. He felt an almost physical pain radiate from his chest. If the baby went, he, Travis, would have no more family ties—or contact with Elizabeth Chapman.

He braced himself against the corridor wall until the doctor walked out the door. Instinct drove him to follow in the man's wake, barely pausing to thrust the flowers at the nurse's station receptionist. "Give these to Ms. Chapman," Travis said.

"You can take them in to her, if you like."

"I've got someone I have to see first," he said over his shoulder as he took off down the hall. He just managed to catch up to the man at the elevator. "May I have a moment of your time, Dr. Goldstein?"

The other man turned around. "I'm afraid I don't have time now. My office is full of patients."

"Doctor, from the conversation I just overheard, *I* don't have much time, either. You and Elizabeth Chapman were discussing some decisions—decisions she has to make within the next couple of days that will radically affect the future of that child."

The doctor's eyes narrowed. "That was a private conversation. Privileged. You had no right—"

Travis saw the hostility in the doctor's eyes. "The child is my brother's son. My name's Travis Logan."

"My condolences, Mr. Logan. Elizabeth told me about your brother and sister-in-law. I liked both Rick and Kathy very much."

"Thank you. I appreciate that. Now, about what Elizabeth was saying—"

"I'm sorry. My answer's still the same. There's nothing I can say. It's privileged information."

"Dr. Goldstein, I'm not asking you to reveal state secrets, or even tell me what her blood pressure is. I just want to know how the hell she has the right to get rid of my brother's child!"

"Come with me," the doctor said, gesturing to an empty room down the hall. "We can talk here. Coffee?" he asked once the door was closed.

"No. No more coffee. I've been living on the stuff." He took a deep breath. "Doctor, I want that child if she doesn't. I'll go to court if I have to."

"You can do that, of course. But you won't get very far. I'm afraid that according to Maryland law, you don't have much of an option. The child belongs to the parents—in this case, Elizabeth. It's all up to her."

"But Elizabeth doesn't want to be a parent."

"Makes no difference," the doctor stated. "The disposition of the child rests solely with Elizabeth Chapman."

"But what about the fact that the baby's father is—was— my brother?"

"That doesn't cut any ice."

Travis felt the doctor's words as a blow, an actual pain in the middle of his chest, over the region of his heart. "We'll see about that," he grated.

"Mr. Logan, there would have to be a home study, interviews. It all takes time. Are you a Maryland resident?"

"No," Travis admitted.

"Then that's another complication."

Maybe he could pay Elizabeth to keep the child until he got approved by the state—work out some arrangement with her, Travis thought. "About the surrogacy contract—"

"Yes, I know about it."

"What happens now?" Travis asked.

"What do you mean?"

"Well, Rick and Kathy aren't here, but this *is* my brother's child. I'm the executor of their wills, and I'm prepared to carry out all the provisions laid out in the codicil. Hell, I'd do it even if it weren't written down in black and white."

"That's admirable, Mr. Logan. But you'll have to take this up with Ms. Chapman, because the surrogacy contract is no longer valid. It states that the child is to be given to Rick and Kathy Logan. Stripped down to its bare essentials, it means that the biological mother is to turn over the child to the biological father."

"And Rick's dead," Travis stated dully. "Then there's no way out?"

"Mr. Logan," the doctor replied gently, "you'll have to talk to Elizabeth Chapman."

"Don't worry, I intend to," Travis said, getting to his feet.

"Just a minute, Logan."

Travis turned, puzzled at the doctor's harsh tone of voice. "What is it?"

"Elizabeth doesn't need any additional stress. She's going to need help and support from somewhere," the doctor warned. "She shouldn't be alone for the next few days. The physical effects of childbirth combined with the emotional trauma of losing her two best friends have dealt a pretty severe shock to her system. And there's nobody I know of who would have cared for her the way Rick and Kathy would have."

"About the custody issue, Doctor—would offering her more money be likely to win me any concessions?"

"More money?" the other man echoed. "That wouldn't be hard to do. It might be hard to get her to accept it, though."

"What does that mean?"

"Elizabeth Chapman became a surrogate for the grand and glorious sum of one dollar."

"A dollar!" Travis gasped, shaking his head in disbelief. "What kind of woman would do that for one dollar?"

"You'll have to ask her. And now, you'll have to excuse me, Mr. Logan," the doctor said, getting to his feet. "I've got a consultation."

"Thank you for your time, Dr. Goldstein," Travis said as the other man walked out the door.

Shock piled up on shock in ever-increasing layers: The death of his family. The knowledge of the child that would never be. The mystery woman who'd given birth to his brother's child. The contract that had named her as a surrogate mother. The realization that money had been the furthest thing from her mind. And then, before he could spare breath to react to all of that, he'd heard her say she was going to give the child away. To strangers. So that his family, newly dead, then reborn, would die again.

As he walked out of the empty room, Travis considered telling Elizabeth that he would pay her to hold off on putting the child up for adoption until his approval as a parent was made official. But he knew that if he came on too strong, he might scare her off. She didn't trust him; she had no reason to.

Feeling much older than his thirty-two years, Travis headed for Elizabeth's room. Stopping just short of the doorway, he noticed how fragile she looked, but knew that certain things would have to be said. His instincts urged him to back away from an emotional involvement he didn't understand. But he couldn't afford to; he sensed he would only have one chance.

EVERY TIME ELIZABETH heard footsteps she jumped, sure that Travis would be walking in the door. He would want to talk about the bombshell she'd dropped on him the night before and she was dreading it. But in spite of everything, she was drawn to him, she realized, unable to conceal the smile on her face as he entered the room.

"Thank you for the flowers," she murmured softly, touched by his thoughtfulness. He looked different somehow, perhaps because now he was clean-shaven and his clothes, though casual—jeans, a thick wool sweater and a down jacket—looked fresh. But now, as she peered up into his face, she was aware that something was very, very wrong.

The hard-eyed stranger was back, she realized instantly, his hazel eyes turning to yellow ice, freezing her as he simply stared back at her. Her smile turned brittle, then faded and died. "What's wrong?" she asked, her voice dry as dust.

"Are you planning to give the baby up for adoption?" he asked without preamble.

"How did you know—"

"I didn't just get here," he admitted. "I came earlier, and as I was coming in, I heard you talking to the doctor about the baby."

"You eavesdropped. You had no right."

"I know that. I didn't mean to. And then when I heard what was being said, I couldn't turn away. I'm sorry, but the subject of the conversation was too important for me to start worrying about etiquette. That baby is all the family I have in the world. I have every right to know what's going on."

She reached for the call button. He moved it out of the way, trapping her hand between his hard palm and the bed underneath. She started to pull against him, grimacing at the discomfort from her stitches.

He quickly backed off, alarmed at her wince of pain and the sudden absence of color in her face. "Are you all right?"

Elizabeth nodded, realizing she couldn't ignore him indefinitely. "Yes," she conceded grudgingly.

"And we can talk about this, Elizabeth? Please?"

Again, she nodded.

"You went to a lot of trouble to have this child. Nine months are gone from your life."

Although he wasn't shouting, she felt the controlled impact of his words. "You're right. It was nine months of *my* life, my pain, my trouble, to have the child. And it was my desire for the child—" and for herself, she added silently, "—to be part of a family, to give him to Rick and Kathy."

"But they're not here now."

"That doesn't change anything. I still want the child to have two parents."

"Just any two people?"

"Of course not! They would be screened. Chosen. Two loving parents."

"It'll take a while to find the right adoptive couple," he reminded her gently, "assuming the right people *can* be found. What happens to the baby in the meantime? He gets stuck in some state-licensed foster home, maybe ends up being transferred from pillar to post. And you can't know what kind of people will eventually adopt him.

"How can you be sure that the right kind of parents will even be on an adoption list? Even if they get past the state adoption authorities, who knows what adoptive parents are really like? You may not even be able to meet them. Or if you do, you'll only be seeing masks."

"What do you mean?"

"You'll see what they want you to see. You can't do that, Elizabeth."

She bridled.

He could tell he was losing her. "Oh, hell. I know you *can.*" Travis realized that logically, her reasons might be unassailable. How could he counter them? What right did he have to counter them? But what choice did he have? "According to your doctor, the law says you can do whatever you want about the child. But I hope you won't."

"Why?"

"Because that child is all the family I have left in the world. Do you know what it means to me to know that there's someone for me to care for—to love?"

"I'm sorry."

"Sorry. You're going to give the baby away and that's all you can say? *Sorry?* What are the options you were discussing with the doctor?"

"I've already told you. Adoption. Foster care."

"Or raising the baby yourself."

"That's not an option."

There was an uncomfortable pause.

"I don't have a choice, Travis."

"There are always choices, Elizabeth." For the first time, he saw a gleam of interest in her eyes.

"Like what?" she asked.

He left the side of the bed abruptly. "Look, let me ask you something, Elizabeth. Is there a man in your life?"

She stared at him in shock. "Why?"

"I'm wondering if you're giving the baby up because a child might be a drain on your social life."

She flushed red, then paled alarmingly. "Travis—"

"You're a beautiful woman," he continued, as if she hadn't spoken. "There might be someone who's objected to the fact you were carrying this child, someone else's child. Maybe he can't tolerate that you bore another man's child, or that the child is part of your life now."

She was still reeling at his description of her as beautiful. "There *is* no man. No one." There hadn't been a man in her life—at least, not on a regular basis—since her marriage to Dennis Chapman had disintegrated.

Travis cleared his throat. "That doesn't mean that there won't be someone in the future, someone who wouldn't be prepared to accept another man's child."

"Forget about my social life. That's not an issue."

"All right, your social life isn't the issue. Then what?"

"It's my right to decide what happens to the child."

"But I *care* about the baby, Elizabeth." And about *you*, he added silently. "I'm prepared to put my life-style on hold until the child is settled."

"This child should be part of a two-parent family right from the start. That's the way the contract was set up. That's what Rick and Kathy wanted. It's what *I* want. And besides, the child isn't part of my life."

"Right," he sneered with a cynical laugh. "I heard you tell the doctor you haven't even seen the baby. If you haven't seen him, how can you give him away?"

"That's why I haven't been to the nursery. It's just—it would be hard to leave him behind if I saw him."

"Then why are you leaving him?"

"I was only carrying the baby. I'm not the one who prepared to be a mother. Kathy did."

"You can become prepared. There are probably classes, vidcos."

"No—just no. Go away, Travis, and leave me alone. I can't take anymore. Not now."

"Please, Elizabeth—" He saw her mouth quiver as she turned her head away from him. "I'll be back."

Why doesn't that surprise me? Her silent question remained unanswered as she watched him walk out of her room.

Concentrating all her efforts, she tried to shut him out but to no avail. There was no escape; her mind was still working, replaying his words. She heard once again the rough emotion in his voice, saw the stiffness of his face, the taut way he'd held himself. She'd been expecting an explosion when she'd told him no. Instead, it had been as if a visor had come down to shield his pain-filled eyes.

There was a depressing feeling of letdown: grief over Rick and Kathy. In addition to them, a third presence lingered in her consciousness: Travis Logan. And a fourth: the child. "You haven't even seen him," Travis had bitten out. "How can you give him away?" The words were trapped in the empty darkness within her.

4

TALKING TO TRAVIS had only caused pain, Elizabeth mused, for both of them. Talking to the doctor hadn't helped at all. She didn't want to talk to a social worker—not yet. And now that Rick and Kathy...

Elizabeth recalled the many evenings she'd spent brainstorming with Kathy Logan. She thought of her own mother who'd rejected, even ridiculed, the whole idea of surrogacy. And then she thought of two people who'd been supportive all along—more supportive in understanding her surrogacy than her own mother had been: Brad and Jenny Fairhall. They might not have the answers to her questions. But they might be willing to lend an ear, give a fresh perspective.

She reached for the bedside telephone, then hesitated warily, feeling awkward about imposing on people who weren't really close friends. And as always, Elizabeth admitted wryly to herself as her damp hand picked up the receiver, she wasn't anxious to admit that she needed help.

When Jenny Fairhall answered the phone, Elizabeth heard the familiar noise of the three Fairhall children in the background, then Jenny's plea for quiet before she came back to the phone slightly breathless, apologizing for the delay. "How are you?"

"I'm—at Garland Memorial. I had the baby."

"Is everything okay?" Jenny asked, sensing an oddness in Elizabeth's voice. "Is the baby all right?"

Elizabeth bit her lip to prevent a sob from escaping. "The— the baby came early. I was at Rick and Kathy's—oh, God..." Her eyes brimmed over as she was no longer able to hold back the tide of tears. "Jenny, could you—come?" To her great relief, the answer was an immediate yes.

"I'll just get Brad to come out of the workshop so he can watch the kids. Do you want me to bring you anything from your house?"

Elizabeth offered up silent thanks that she and the Fairhalls had exchanged keys when they'd "housewatched" for each other. "If it's not too much trouble, could you stop by and pick up my suitcase for me? It's by the front door."

"Sure. What's your room number at the hospital?"

"It's room 412. I'll leave your name with the security guard on the maternity floor."

"WHAT HAPPENED?" Jenny Fairhall asked as she walked into Elizabeth's room forty-five minutes later and set the suitcase on the floor by the bed.

Elizabeth had an almost dizzying sense of déjà vu as she looked into Jenny's soft, questioning brown eyes and tried to formulate an answer. Now she understood how Travis must have felt when he'd had to tell her about Rick's and Kathy's deaths. After a futile effort to clear her throat, she simply drew a shuddering breath and said the words.

Shock and sympathy transformed Jenny's features as she sat down on the edge of the bed and gathered the other woman into her arms. "I am so sorry. I don't know what to say. . . ." And then, aware of the rigidity in Elizabeth's body, Jenny murmured, "Let it go, honey. It's okay to cry."

"I can't. I'll be all right," Elizabeth said hoarsely, grateful for the hug. "I—I'm getting used to the idea, or at least, I tell myself I am. It's just—the words are still hard to get out." They were even hard to think about, she admitted to herself.

"I know they meant the world to you. You should have called me. I hate to think of your being alone when you found out about Rick and Kathy, and then going into labor. I would have come immediately."

"I wasn't alone. Rick's brother, Travis, was the one that told me about them. He drove me to the hospital and stayed with me until after the baby was born."

Jenny's eyes widened when she saw the color that briefly flooded Elizabeth's pale cheeks at the mention of Rick Logan's brother. "What's he like?"

"He's—I mean he's—we've had our disagreements." Elizabeth broke off, too tired to rehash her argument with Travis. At the same time, she couldn't bring herself to be too hard on him. She was his direct link to Rick and Kathy, just as he was her link to them.

"So tell me about the baby," Jenny suggested when Elizabeth said nothing further. And when the other woman didn't answer, Jenny tried again, this time changing the subject. "Every time I've given birth, the nurses have practically routed me out of bed with dire threats. How about you?"

"They do want me to do some walking," Elizabeth conceded.

"Okay, then," Jenny said brightly, "why don't I help you get your 'workout' by walking down to the nursery with you so you can show me the baby?" As Jenny looked on, Elizabeth's face seemed to turn a shade paler.

She shook her head violently. "I can't."

"You're not well enough?" And when Elizabeth said nothing, "Look, I just—I know all of this must be hard for you. And don't feel you have to tell me anything if you don't want to. I'm here to help you and offer support, not to make you more miserable than you already are."

"I'm scared, Jenny. Scared."

"Of what?"

"Of seeing him. The baby."

"Elizabeth, all new mothers have worries. Heck, even mothers with lots of practice get frown lines and gray hairs." Then in an effort to stem the tide of Elizabeth's anguish, she added softly, "Even if the baby won't know his father, he'll have his mother and his uncle."

Elizabeth's desperate battle to maintain her fragile self-control was finally shattered as the tears that she'd been holding back overflowed. "No, he won't."

"Rick's brother—this Travis Logan—hasn't been supportive? He's not interested in his brother's son? He must be a jerk!"

"He's not a jerk. *I'm* the one with the problem. I just can't handle it. I don't know what's the right thing to do."

"What right thing, Elizabeth?"

"About keeping the baby. That's what Travis and I argued about. I want to put the baby up for adoption, and Travis is against that idea. And I'm scared that if I see the baby, I won't be able to give him up," she blurted out. "You think I'm a terrible person, don't you? Or at least, a wimp," Elizabeth said, turning away from her friend.

"No, of course I don't," Jenny said, then paused, knowing she would have to choose her words carefully. "You've been through a lot—physically, psychologically, and emotionally. No one can blame you for feeling rocky—for being afraid to be on the high wire without a net below you. But don't you think maybe you're too overwrought to make such a serious decision right now?" Jenny took a deep breath. "Let's back up a bit. Have you seen the baby at all?"

"Just after he was born."

"Look, Elizabeth, I'm not going to try to tell you what to do. No one has that right. But is it right to give this baby away without even looking at him? Don't you think you should at least see him? Once you give him away, it may be too late to change your mind."

"Other mothers give their babies up for adoption."

"Other mothers aren't in your situation," Jenny replied. "You've had to deal with Rick's and Kathy's deaths. You have to psychologically undo all that careful planning—the baby you thought would be Kathy's is now yours. And the physiological trauma of childbirth knocks your hormones out of whack. Not to mention having to contend with Rick's brother." And then, to soften the harshness of her words, "Why not take it one step at a time? Why don't we just take that walk to the nursery?"

"What if I fall in love with him?" Elizabeth asked as she and Jenny slowly left the room.

Jenny had to dig deep to frame an answer. "Then you'll be better equipped to base your decision on what's best for the baby, rather than letting your fears dictate to you. If you love the child and *then* decide to give him up, at least you know you'll be doing what you think is best for him."

With Jenny at her side, Elizabeth made her way slowly down the hospital corridor, her heart pounding like a jackhammer when she finally reached the doorway of the nursery. Peering through the glass, she saw several rows of bassinets. One of them held her son.

She hovered at the threshold of the nursery in an agony of indecision.

"You don't have to go in," Jenny said quietly. "One of the nurses can simply show you where he is."

Taking a deep breath, Elizabeth went into the nursery, with Jenny walking behind.

While Elizabeth waited, the nurse went to an isolette on the far side of the room and came back with a blue-blanketed bundle. Paralyzed by a bewildering barrage of emotions, Elizabeth was treated to a too-brief demonstration of the best way to hold a newborn: cuddle close, always supporting the baby's head with the palm of one hand, his bottom with the other. She froze, making no move to take the child from the nurse's arms.

"Hi, sweetheart," Jenny crooned, edging closer to the child in the hopes that Elizabeth would venture nearer, too. "It's a big world out here, huh? All kinds of new people to meet.

Like this lady, here." She gave Elizabeth's hand a slight squeeze. "They don't bite, you know, Elizabeth. At least, not at this stage," Jenny added facetiously.

"I'm relieved to hear that," Elizabeth responded, not taking her eyes off the child.

"And they like to be held," Jenny added in soft-voiced tones of encouragement.

"Can I—hold him?" Elizabeth asked the nurse hesitantly.

"Of course," came the reply.

As the child was given to her, Elizabeth tried to remember the instructions she'd just been given. He was so small, she marveled, yet he seemed to fill the emptiness in her tensely waiting arms.

She was suffused with a rare feeling of wonder, privilege and humility at being able to hold this child who was the product of so much love—her love for Rick and Kathy; their love for each other and for their child. For *her* child. In that frozen moment in time, she was overwhelmed, moved beyond words by a tide of feelings she couldn't begin to understand.

Her hold on the fragile bundle tightened automatically as pent-up emotions overflowed and tears streamed down her cheeks. When she could finally see through her tears, it seemed to her that she could see Rick's features in that tiny face. She noticed the baby's coppery wisps of hair and thought of her own hair, wondering if this child—her child— would hear the taunt she'd heard so often while growing up: carrot top.

Is this how all mothers felt? Is this what Kathy would have felt, Elizabeth asked herself as she handed the baby back to the nurse moments later.

After Jenny left, she spent most of the rest of the night trying to answer that question.

THE NEXT MORNING she woke up exhausted from thinking about the child she had held so briefly the night before.

His image stayed with her as she mechanically ate breakfast, showered and changed into the silky turquoise robe Jenny had brought. And then she walked back to the nursery to see him, not going inside this time, but staying on the outside looking in.

It was a position that was familiar to her, she realized, summing up all her insecurities. As she peered unseeingly into the nursery, it seemed as if she had spent the greater part of her life on the other side of the glass. As a child, as an adult, even as a married woman, she'd seen life from the other side, as an observer, not as a participant—with a metaphorical pane of glass separating her from everything else. Alone against the world.

Her surrogacy arrangement had been her way of being part of a family—a perfect family. Now, because of circumstances, she was once more on the outside looking in.

And only she had the power to change her life, she realized.

By late afternoon she had a pounding headache, the result of questions unanswered, decisions unmade. "To keep or not to keep?" she muttered under her breath in an odd parody of Hamlet's soliloquy. Maybe a change of scene would help, she thought, as she made her way down the corridor to the solarium and sank down gratefully into the softness of an overstuffed couch.

Leaning her head back and closing her eyes, she recalled her conversation with Dr. Goldstein, with Jenny, all the while asking herself for the thousandth time what Rick and Kathy would have wanted. And then she remembered the hurt and pain on Travis's face when he'd confronted her about her wanting to put the child up for adoption.

EVERY TIME TRAVIS SAW Elizabeth Chapman, he discovered a different facet of her, as if he were meeting her for the first time. From his first encounter with a carefree pregnant lady to the new mother who, ravaged by physical and emotional torment, had denied her own child.

Now, as he entered the solarium at the end of the long hallway, he discovered yet another image of Elizabeth. She was sitting on a sofa, her blue-green robe splashed with a brilliant design, her vibrant auburn hair gathered back from her delicate features by a twist of ribbons.

"Travis!" she gasped, galvanized by the way he'd virtually materialized just as she'd been thinking of him. She rose to her feet, swaying slightly.

"Hello, Elizabeth," he greeted, his strong hands automatically clasping her shoulders to steady her. As she stood supported by his two hands, he saw the still-rounded figure that was no longer pregnant, the crystalline eyes reflecting surprise at his presence—and a mouth that seemed to have forgotten how to smile.

She stared up at him, wondering what had changed, what had made him look different, somehow. Though he still seemed tense and weary, the hard edge that had been a part of him was no longer there. "I haven't come to a decision—"

"That's not why I'm here," he cut in quickly. "At least, not exactly. This hasn't been easy for either one of us. I spent most of last night walking the floor." *Walking the floors of that damned, empty house.* At least thinking of Elizabeth had temporarily pried his mind away from thoughts of Rick and Kathy. "I thought maybe we could sit down and talk. Just—talk."

"All right," she replied, sitting down again, her hands tightly clasped in her lap. He sat down next to her.

"I came to offer you an alternative, Elizabeth—to—" His throat worked as he forced himself to continue. "To giving the baby up for adoption."

"I don't *have* an alternative."

He covered her hands with his own. "We could work something out, you and I."

"I don't see what," she whispered, mesmerized by the hands that covered hers, resting in the cradle of her thighs.

"You could give him to me."

"You!" She dislodged his hands from hers, startled at the intensity of her feelings—compassion, disbelief, and a wariness that bordered on dread. "It wouldn't work for you to have the baby. You're a bachelor. You have no experience. You're not prepared. You don't know anything about raising a child."

"The same could be said for you or for any new parent. Besides, why are you objecting? You're going to give him away to people you don't even know—people Rick and Kathy didn't know. How can you do that? Hell, you haven't even seen him, or given him a name—"

"I have seen him," she cut in. "Yesterday."

"You—how was he?"

"Fine."

"And the name? Have you given him a name?"

She shook her head.

"Elizabeth, let me have him if you don't want him."

"You live in Connecticut. I signed an agreement that I would give the child to Rick and Kathy." Suppressing a sob, she held herself back from saying that she was to have been part of the "family" also. "I'm not about to give him up to a man I barely know, who doesn't even maintain a home. You're hardly ever home at all. Kathy used to call you a high-tech nomad."

"I have a home, a perfectly respectable condominium in Connecticut. I'll get a housekeeper."

She sat straighter, her chest heaving. "There's just no way I'd let you take that baby off to some sterile environment. The reason I went through all this was to give the child to two loving parents, not to one impersonal housekeeper and an absentee uncle."

"Then you care about the baby, Elizabeth?"

"Of course I care!"

"Caught you out, didn't I?"

"Don't be so smug, Travis. Just because I care doesn't mean that I'm emotionally equipped to be a parent."

"Neither am I. Look, why don't you give it a try? You can always change your mind." He paused, his voice so tight with emotion that he could barely continue. "You can always give him up."

"I—I don't think that would be possible." She took a deep breath, striving for calm. "I think we've both said enough, more than enough for now. Why don't we just call it a day?"

"Try it. *Please*," he begged, hoping his plea would penetrate the virtually impenetrable mask that seemed to have dropped over her face. "My brother's son is someone to care for. He's all that's left of my family." Yet even as he said the words, Travis realized that because of her almost mysterious connection with Rick and Kathy, Elizabeth was part of his family, too. "If I could just make you understand . . ."

"I'm sorry, Travis," she said huskily.

"If he's adopted, I'll never see him again."

She swallowed hard, struggling to conceal her reaction to his words. At the back of her mind was the concern that *she* might never see the baby again, either. "I just want things to be the way they were."

"They can't be that way. You know that, Elizabeth. Things can't be the same again for either one of us. I'm going to sell the town house, and put the money in a trust fund for the child. If you decide to keep the baby, you won't have any financial worries, either. As a computer consultant, I've been pulling in a pretty good salary and I've invested quite a bit of it. I also inherited money from my father." And from Rick's estate, he couldn't quite bring himself to add. "I don't know what it is you do for a living, but I'll compensate you for staying home with the child and not carrying on with your career, whatever that is."

He didn't know who or what she was, Elizabeth thought angrily, or why she'd done what she did. Yet to Travis, it could all be reduced to dollars and cents. "I'm a woodworker."

"Ah, that explains it."

"Explains what?"

He picked up her right hand and gently traced the roughened pads of her fingers.

"Sandpaper and splinters," she said, her hand trembling slightly as she backed away from the warmth of his touch. "My pieces sell in galleries and to buyers in major retail stores. I get well paid for what I do. I make a good living. I can afford to take care of my responsibilities. And I didn't do this for money," she said tersely, trying to get the words past the jagged ache in her throat.

"I realize that. If you had, there wouldn't be a one dollar fee written into the contract. Look, you don't want to make a decision like this under pressure. You keep the baby for now. I'll resettle here. If you—and the state—approve, I'll take him."

"I can't deal with this now. I don't want to talk about it anymore. Not now. It hurts even when I think." She shuddered, struggling for control as the intensity of the argument strained her already taut emotions to the snapping point. "And I won't change my mind—about two parents," she managed, the words caught in a throat rough with tears.

"Don't," he groaned, the sight of the tears coursing down her cheeks tearing him apart. She was shocked when, instead of continuing to be argumentative, he took her into his arms, cradling her close to him, crooning reassurances.

"Don't cry. It'll be all right. We'll figure something out." And then he added, "I'm sorry, Elizabeth. I was wrong to upset you. Forgive me?"

She shrugged, hating the fact that she was once more vulnerable to this man she barely knew.

"I shouldn't have pushed, Elizabeth. I made a mistake. Hasn't that ever happened to you?"

Yes, she'd made mistakes. The biggest one had been getting involved with Dennis Chapman, in the hope that with him, she'd find the love and support she'd never received from her parents when she was growing up. "Sure, I've made my share. And then some."

"Can't you allow me the same privilege, then?"

His voice was barely audible, and his eyes had changed from crystal hardness to velvet softness.

"Yes," she whispered, averting her gaze.

He eased away slightly, so that he could look down into her face. "Can we start over, try being friends, maybe? I'd like to win your trust."

She felt his arm slide away from her back, then saw him extend his hand to her, palm up. She looked down at his hand, then back to his face, which was a mosaic of weariness, grief. There was also a rather touching hint of vulnerability, as if he had warily let his guard down. Whatever it was, it made her want to chance trusting him.

She placed her hand in his.

He closed his other hand over it; then, to her amazement, he lifted her hand to his lips.

She was shivering in anticipation, her heart beating in double time by the time the kiss ended. But even after it was over, the fragile spell of warmth held as he drew her once more into the closeness of his arms.

The gentle Travis was really back again. One large hand cradled the back of her head, the other stroked her back. Her face was nestled into the crisp cotton of his shirt. And with each breath she took, she inhaled his clean, masculine scent.

His embrace was not demanding, not sexually intimate; it was comforting, all the way through to her soul. She couldn't remember the last time someone had held her with such tenderness. She would have liked to remain in his arms, just as she was, for an infinite period of time. But she was not the only one who had suffered terrible loss. Travis, too, had had a part of his life ripped away. He was in pain, and grieving. Yet who was there for him?

Suddenly, she wanted very much to give comfort, as well as take it. As if of their own volition, her palms inched up his chest to his shoulders, her fingers linking behind his neck. She held him as tightly as she could. She heard his breath catch, then felt his arms tighten around her as the warmth of his heartfelt sigh caressed her cheek....

Elizabeth felt so warm and soft and utterly feminine in his arms that for a moment Travis thought only of the acute pleasure her nearness gave him. He forgot where he was and the reason her arms were around him, holding him. He wanted only to follow his impulses and his instincts, and lose himself in her.

A voice on the hospital intercom brought him up short. Reality hit him again. How could he think that about her? he asked himself in disgust. *She's a new mother. The last thing she's probably thinking about is sex.*

He took a deep breath. "Do you have to make a decision about the baby today?"

"Before I leave the hospital tomorrow," she said, the words muffled against his shirt. "I'm sorry."

"We both need time. I know that until now, I haven't been family-oriented." He shook his head. "I always knew they'd be there—Rick and Kathy, I mean. Damn, I was selfish. I took them for granted. I know how precious that infant is. I can assure you that I won't be taking things for granted again.

"And I realize that I certainly don't have the most stable home environment. Maybe you're right. Maybe I'm not the daddy type. Maybe I'd make a lousy father. But I don't want to quit before I've even started."

He took a deep breath. "Be a temporary mother, Elizabeth. Keep the baby for a little while, until I can get settled. Give me a chance to prove to you that I can share in taking care of him." *That I can take care of both of you*, he begged silently, readily acknowledging that as well as having the baby to worry about, there was also the vulnerable woman he held against his heart to consider.

"Travis—"

"I won't browbeat you anymore."

As he eased gradually away from her, he was reluctant to let her go, not wanting to face how empty his arms would feel without her. "I'll pick you up when it's time for you to go home tomorrow," he murmured, his hands still stroking her.

"That isn't necessary. I can get a cab."

"It *is* necessary," he told her gently but firmly. "And I have no ulterior motive. I'll be doing it because I want to, not because it might make you change your mind." He felt she needed his help, and he wanted to give it. "And will you call your friend Jenny? You might need some help the first few days you're home."

She nodded, her cheek rubbing against his chest. Somehow, she couldn't ignore his softly spoken words combined with his strong yet gentle hold on her. "I'll think about what you want."

"Thank you," he said, breathing a sigh of relief. "I won't badger you. But if you want anything or need anything, even if it's just to talk, I'm there for you." With great reluctance, he relinquished his hold on her, guiding her back to the sofa. Once she was seated, he leaned forward, bracing his hands on the back of the sofa, at either side of her slender neck. "Get some rest, Elizabeth." And then, as if it were the most natural thing in the world to do, he bent his head, dropping a kiss on her forehead.

Elizabeth watched Travis hesitate briefly, then leave the solarium. But long after the sounds of his footsteps had faded into silence, his presence stayed with her. It had been so long since she'd been held. When had she *ever* been held in that tender, masculine way? she asked herself. And his kiss was something she savored.

There was so much to think about. Over the course of the afternoon and evening, she visited the nursery more than once. Sometimes she just peered through the glass. Other times, she held the baby. But always, she was drawn to the child by an invisible bond that she couldn't understand—a bond that grew inexorably stronger each time she held him in her arms. And still she was no closer to a decision than before. She only knew that every time she picked him up, it was harder to put him down.

"It's scary," Elizabeth whispered as she visited the nursery for the third time that day, almost too frightened to try to take a deep breath.

"Yes," the nurse agreed, "but it's pretty wonderful, too. Would you like to feed him? It's about that time."

"Could I?"

"Absolutely. Sit down in the armchair."

When Elizabeth had settled into the chair, the nurse showed her how to feed the tiny, helpless child. "Hi, little one," Elizabeth whispered as she bottle-fed her son.

"He doesn't have a name yet," the nurse pointed out gently.

Elizabeth didn't hesitate. "Richard. I'm going to call him Richard. After his father."

"Would you like to have him in your room with you?"

"Can I?"

"Sure."

Elizabeth walked slowly back to her room. Within the half hour, the baby was brought to her. She lay on the bed, gently holding the child in the curve of her arm. Everything about him was a cause for wonder—the tiny round face, the fuzz of red hair, the pinkness of his skin. She was fascinated by the occasional smile, the gurgling sounds, and by the newness of it all. And then, in her mind, she heard the echo of Travis's words, "I'm there for you." She had a strange compulsion to hear his voice. . . .

NEARLY ASLEEP, Travis almost imagined that he was hearing things as he groped for the phone. "H'lo?"

"T—Travis?"

He sat up straight in bed, his fingers tightening around the receiver. "Elizabeth? What's wrong?"

"Nothing. I just—" She looked down at the sleeping child beside her, "—I've been spending more time in the nursery."

He went very still.

"Travis?"

"I'm here."

"I'll do what you want, Travis. I'll—keep him for a while. Temporarily. Then you can take him."

"Thank you," he said, breathing a fervent sigh of relief.

"And Travis, we'll need something for the baby to wear on the way home. If you go into his room at the house, you'll find some baby clothes." She closed her eyes for a moment, remembering. "What we'll need is the bunting. Oh, and a couple of nightshirts. You'll find them in the top drawer of the changing table. The other things can wait till tomorrow."

"What's a bunting?" he asked blankly.

"It's yellow and green, quilted, has a zipper, and it's closed at the bottom, kind of like a sack."

"How do you know about this sack thing?" he asked.

"Kathy and I indulged in a major league shopping spree, and we put it all away."

"I'm sorry," he said gruffly. "I shouldn't have asked."

She could hear strain and discomfort in his voice. "It's all right, Travis. It's not your fault. Don't worry about it."

"Thanks, Elizabeth. I'll be back in the morning to take you—both of you—home."

Home, away from the ordered sterility of the hospital environment that blanked her senses into frozen numbness. She ached to be in her own place, in her own bed, away from pale green walls, starched uniforms, hospital corners, and frayed thermal blankets. Perhaps at home she'd be able to forget what had happened. Then she looked at the baby sleeping so peacefully in his bassinet, and knew that she would never forget.

5

AFTER HANGING UP the phone, Travis lay back in bed, his body stiff with a curious mixture of tension and euphoria that was compounded by the knowledge that he'd never thought of fatherhood as a role for himself. Yes, he'd wanted the child. But in his own mind he couldn't separate the child from Elizabeth.

She and the child were irrevocably joined, even if Elizabeth didn't think so. He didn't want to lose her. And now there was no doubt that his connection with her, however tenuous, would continue, at least temporarily. For some reason, the thought excited him.

Travis stumbled out of bed feeling nearly drugged with lack of sleep, but elated at the same time. Certainly, he felt relief. But then, reality set in. He went down to the desk in the study and looked up the number of Rick's lawyer, Philip Snyder. Travis had called the man earlier in the day to inform him of Rick's and Kathy's deaths. Now, despite the lateness of the hour, he called the lawyer back.

After apologizing to the attorney for waking him up, Travis told him about the agreement that had been reached with Elizabeth regarding the adoption of the baby.

"Is she sure about this?" Philip Snyder asked.

"Yes," Travis answered tensely.

"Not that I mind calls from clients at any time, but is there any urgent reason for this midnight call?"

"I guess you could say I'm overreacting, Mr. Snyder, but I want to make sure that the baby's future is assured. I don't want to leave things to chance. As I've learned to my cost—

in Rick and Kathy's case. I guess you could say I want to make
sure matters are arranged in case—God forbid—anything
should happen."

"All right, Mr. Logan. I can see where you're coming from.
And I can start the paperwork that would set adoption proceedings in motion. But I want you to know, it won't happen
overnight. Court dockets are notoriously crowded."

"I'm not in any hurry," Travis replied. "I just want to get
things started. Is there anything I have to sign?"

"We'll get to that when we get a lot closer to things being
finalized."

Travis's hand shook as he replaced the receiver in the cradle. Once he was in bed again, sleep seemed very far away.
He was about to gain his objective: he was keeping his
brother's son. It was the best solution all around. He should
have been ecstatic. He was getting what he wanted. *Or was
he?*

For so long, he had led an isolated, insular existence, with
no one to depend on, and no one to depend on him. He'd been
in control of an empty existence where work was the only
constant. Now that Elizabeth and a child had come into his
life, things were happening—spinning out of control—at an
ever-increasing rate. As he courted sleep once more, he uttered a silent prayer that he would be equal to the challenge....

TRAVIS WAS DUE at the hospital at 10:30 a.m. Elizabeth was
determined to be ready for him. Having showered, she dusted
lightly with scented powder, then donned her loose-fitting,
cream-colored slacks and a navy pullover sweater.

She gave her hair a good brushing and secured it with a
ribbon. After that, she applied a light touch of makeup—
tawny lipstick and mascara—and felt decidedly more human.

While she was waiting for Travis, she called Dr. Goldstein and told him that she wouldn't be needing a visit from the hospital social worker.

"I'm glad you're keeping the child, Elizabeth. I think you'll be good for each other."

She heaved a shaky sigh. "Thank you. And I'll be using the pediatrician Rick and Kathy selected." She made no mention of the tentative nature of the arrangement with Travis.

Then her thoughts shifted to Travis Logan. She found herself excited about his picking her up, almost as if she were a girl on her first date.

ELIZABETH LOOKED UP, sensing Travis's presence. He was standing in the doorway, wearing a down parka over jeans, a heavy sweater, and boots. He was carrying the bunting and nightshirts on one arm, as well as her own down jacket, from the town house. She took a deep breath. "Come in."

Travis walked into the room and froze, his gaze swinging from the woman sitting on the side of the bed, to the bassinet, and back again.

"Hi," she said as evenly as she could.

"Hi. I don't know if I'm early, or late, or what happens next. I—"

"Come say hello," she encouraged softly, nodding toward the bassinet.

His face was working, his eyes blurred as he crossed the room and peered down at the sleeping child. "He's beautiful," Travis said, his voice a husky whisper.

"Do you want to hold him?"

"I'd love to."

She leaned down to pick up the baby and lifted him out of the bassinet with painstaking care, recalling her own introduction to the child in the nursery. "Um, I think it might be better if you sat down," she suggested, nodding her head toward the vinyl armchair.

Travis tossed the bunting onto the bed, then sat down in the chair and waited, his heartbeat accelerating with Elizabeth's every move. It looked as if she were carrying a doll dressed in a blue nightshirt. And then she leaned over, about to place the tiny bundle in his waiting arms. His brother's son.

"Wait!" he hissed in a strangled whisper.

"What's wrong?" she asked.

"I've never done this before."

He looked absolutely petrified, she thought tenderly. "Well, you're not exactly talking to the voice of experience, here."

"I'll bet you're a quick study."

"Travis!"

"Right." He swallowed, looking up at her. "What now?"

"Make a loose cradle of your arms." When he'd done so, she carefully placed the infant in his arms. "Now, your right hand goes under his bottom, the other—" He was looking up at her, a blank stare in his eyes. She slid her hand under his, to move it into the proper position. She bit her lip, as her hand inadvertently touched Travis's lap. "I'm sorry," she gasped, knowing her cheeks were flushed. Then she berated herself for calling attention to her own stupidity.

"Elizabeth," he said softly, forcing himself to tamp down his immediate physical reaction to the unconscious intimacy of her touch.

Unable to do anything else, she looked down at him.

"It's all right," he told her.

His voice was slow and steady, with no trace of mockery, his attitude one of patient waiting.

Get on with it, she ordered herself sternly as she moved Travis's left hand until his large palm was cradling the back of the baby's head.

"Thank you."

Her retreat stopped when the back of her knees hit the side of the bed.

A kaleidoscope of conflicting emotions whirled through him with dizzying rapidity. Fear. Bitterness and profound grief that he, Travis, was a miserably inadequate substitute for his brother. Joy and wonder for the featherweight miracle that, thanks to the woman sitting near him, he held in his trembling arms.

Tears came to Elizabeth's eyes as she watched him.

"He looks a little like Rick, don't you think?" Travis asked, his eyes misting over.

"Yes," she said, wiping away a tear of her own, watching Travis all the while.

"And like you, Elizabeth," he said softly. "He has your coppery hair."

She nodded, too full of emotion to speak.

"About a name—"

"Richard," she replied huskily. "I named him Richard."

Travis could only nod, unable to get any words past the constriction in his throat. Every muscle frozen in place, he concentrated on doing nothing to disturb the child. Furthermore, if he did nothing, surely he could do nothing wrong. He hoped. How long he might have stayed that way, he had no idea. Elizabeth's voice broke the spell.

"How are you doing?"

"Aside from being paralyzed, you mean?" he asked with a wry smile.

"That's just the way I felt at first. Ready for a break?"

"Yeah," he said, heaving a great sigh.

Taking a deep breath, Elizabeth lifted the child from Travis's arms. "Are you okay to stay here with him for a while?" she asked as she placed the infant in the bassinet.

Startled, he looked up at her, then across at the child. "Where are you going?"

"To pay the hospital bill."

"It's already been paid."

Her eyes narrowed. "I pay my own way, Travis."

"I never doubted that for a moment. Look, you're tired and so am I. Can't this discussion wait until later?" Reading her glare to mean no, he sank back into the chair. "Elizabeth, does your health insurance cover surrogacy?"

"No."

"And Rick was—involved." To his amusement he saw her blush.

"Yes," she hissed. "Of course he was *involved*."

"And you were the surrogate. Weren't Rick and Kathy going to pay your medical expenses?"

"Yes," she admitted. "But—"

"Well, I'm Rick's surrogate," he cut in quietly. "I paid the bill because he's not here to do it. Now can we go home?"

She couldn't help smiling. He sounded for all the world like a whiny child. "Yes, Travis."

"Do you have anything to take with you?" he asked, his eyes trained on Elizabeth as she slid the baby into the bunting and zipped it shut.

She shook her head. "Just the suitcase and the baby's goody bag. Let's go *home*."

She said the word as if it were an incantation, Travis noted. It made him wonder. "Where's home, Elizabeth?"

"Off of Charles Street, about four miles from here."

They made an awkward procession: Elizabeth was seated in the requisite wheelchair with the baby on her lap. Travis was holding the suitcase and the goody bag of baby powder, diapers, bottles of ready-to-use formula in one hand and the car seat in the other.

As Travis threaded the car through the hospital garage, Elizabeth, sitting in the back seat, looked down at Ritchie. He was asleep, and so bundled up against the cold that not much more than his nose was visible.

"Elizabeth."

Travis's voice cut into her thoughts. She looked at him quizzically, wondering why the car hadn't progressed beyond the end of the hospital driveway. "Is something wrong?" she asked him.

"I need directions. I'm not exactly on home turf."

"Oh, sorry. Turn right here at the end of the driveway, then left at the second light."

Elizabeth's directions led him to a residential area replete with tree-lined streets, landscaped grounds, and massive homes that could arguably be called mansions. His eyes widened in disbelief as she directed him to turn into a long, winding driveway that led to one of the largest houses he'd ever seen. He flicked a sideways glance at her. "*This* is where you live?" he asked incredulously.

She wasn't surprised that he'd reached that conclusion. "Not exactly," she murmured, then told him to keep following the driveway. Finally, she told him to stop. "*This* is where I live. Where I rent, actually."

What he saw was a building dwarfed by the massive house he'd seen earlier. It was a two-story cottage house, made of fieldstone and trimmed with wood that created a tudor effect. It was small, snug, and utterly charming—the exact opposite of what he'd expected. He'd thought that since she was a single woman, she'd probably live in an apartment or condo.

As they got out of the car, Elizabeth carried the goody bag, while Travis took charge of the car seat, complete with baby. "We'll take it slowly," he said as they walked up the slate pathway to the front door.

As she walked at Travis's side to the carriage house where she'd lived for two years, she was aware of a subtle undercurrent of uneasiness. For some reason, the house didn't feel the same anymore. As she unlocked the heavy front door and pushed it open, she felt like a stranger. She'd worked so hard to make this into a home, and now it felt as if she didn't belong here.

"Elizabeth, is something wrong?" he asked at her apparent reluctance to go into the house.

She gave herself a mental shake. "No. Yes. Come in."

Once they were inside, he seated her in an oversize armchair. Then he asked where he should put the baby.

"On the floor next to me, where I can see him."

"There you go, little guy," Travis murmured as he set the car seat gently on the floor next to Elizabeth. "I'll just go back out to the car and get your suitcase. Where do you want it?" he asked.

"Just through that doorway on the daybed," she gestured as she took off her down jacket and dropped it on the nearby sofa. "That's the 'finishing room,' where I usually do fine work on small woodworking projects." In addition to the quilt-covered daybed, the room also included a television, an audio system and a small worktable.

In the brief time that it took Travis to retrieve the suitcase and deposit it in her room, Elizabeth waited silently, her hands clenched in her lap.

Travis would be leaving now. She pulled herself together with effort, determined not to show her disappointment. "Thank you for everything you've done. You've been very kind."

"Save the speeches for later, Elizabeth. I want you to tell me what's bothering you."

"I'm irresponsible, that's what's bothering me. I don't have any formula or diapers, other than what we brought with us from the hospital. There's no bottle warmer—"

"You are *not* irresponsible."

"But I should have thought of this."

"Elizabeth, since you had the baby three weeks early, there was no need to buy formula. And even under the best of circumstances, you couldn't very well buy the stuff until the pediatrician at the hospital told you what kind to get, now could you?"

"No, I guess not," she admitted grudgingly.

"All right, then. You sit back and relax and keep an eye on the little one. I'll be back in a while."

"You will?"

"Did you really think I was going to abandon you? No, don't answer that. I don't think I want to know. I'm going shopping. To get some things for the baby. Can I borrow your house keys? I don't want you to have to get up to open the door when I come back. You might be asleep."

"Not likely! I don't think being stranded with a newborn baby is conducive to sleep."

"Probably not," Travis agreed with a wry smile. "Now, how about putting together a short list for me?" he asked, whipping a small leather notebook out of his pocket.

"Um, I don't think you need to buy too much. A couple of cans of the recommended formula, a box of diapers, Baby Wipes, a bottle warmer. Oh, and some bottles—three or four should do, I guess. That should hold us until we can figure out exactly what we need. The keys are in my jacket pocket," she said. "And Travis—thank you."

"Hey, we're in this together, remember? I'll go to the supermarket I passed near Rick's house. And don't worry about fixing a meal, either. I'll take care of that, too."

"You don't have to do that."

"Hey, I want to." And then he crouched down in front of the car seat and gazed down at the still-sleeping baby, then back up at Elizabeth. "He looks so contented," Travis said, his voice tinged with wonder. "He didn't mind the car ride at all."

As he got to his feet, he looked down at the baby once more, then back at Elizabeth.

"Sit back and relax," he urged. "I'll be back soon." And then he bent down and pressed his lips to Elizabeth's forehead.

"What was that for?" she asked, staring up at him.

"For Ritchie," Travis said, the barest outline of a smile twitching at his lips. "See you later Elizabeth. Bye-bye, Ritchie."

"'Bye, Travis," she echoed softly as he walked out the door.

More than a little bemused from Travis's kiss, Elizabeth turned her attention back to the baby, who was still wrapped in the quilted bunting. She drew a deep breath. "Oh, Ritchie," she murmured softly, "you're all bundled up for the outside. You must be too warm."

Wiping slightly damp hands on her sweats, she bent toward the car seat. "Maybe I should wait until Travis gets back." She bit her lip. "Coward. You picked Ritchie up in the hospital. You fed him. Heck, you even changed him. You're an old hand. Pretend you're back there now and you're lifting him out of the bassinet. Yeah. Right."

She released the safety strap, and very gingerly picked Ritchie up. She held her breath, but he didn't awaken. Instead, he settled right onto her lap. "So far so good," she muttered. With great care, she unzipped the bunting. But before she could lift him away from it, he started thrashing his little arms and legs and screaming.

"Oh, no!" she exclaimed, scooping him up into her arms and cuddling him against her shoulder. "I should have left you in the bunting. I should have waited for Travis. But then you would have become overheated. Shh. That's a good boy. Shh. Oh, God," she moaned. "What do I do now?"

Still clasping the squalling baby to her shoulder, she got up, searching frantically for the goody bag. Maybe he was hungry, she decided. She tried to juggle Ritchie, holding him securely, all the while rummaging through the bag for a bottle of formula. Eventually, she ran out of hands and had to put him back into the car seat.

And all the while he was screaming, his little face pitifully contorted.

Finally, she got the ready-made bottle and hurried back to the chair, where she picked up the baby, nestled him into the crook of her arm and put the bottle to his mouth. It worked! She exulted. Like magic, the crying stopped. As he sucked the nipple, the scrunches in his face melted into chubby roundness. His little fists stopped flailing the air.

When Ritchie had drunk the first ounce of the bottle, she cautiously eased it from his tiny fingers. Then she gently patted his back hoping for a burp, which finally happened—on her shoulder. She wrinkled her nose at the pungent smell, remembering too late what she'd been told in the hospital—"Always drape a cloth over your shoulder when you burp the infant."

Shaking her head, she gave him the bottle again, letting him suck until it was nearly empty. Then she burped him again, this time reaching for a dish towel first. She headed back to the living room, intending to put Ritchie back into the car seat for now.

To her surprise, she couldn't bring herself to put him down. Instead, she sat down with him in her arms, gently rocking him back and forth.

And then the real reason flashed across her mind like the tail of a comet. She hadn't returned him to the car seat because she liked the way Ritchie felt in her arms, as if he were a part of her. She was so shaken by the thought that she could barely keep her arms from trembling as she finally eased him back into the car seat.

"Pull yourself together," she ordered herself. "Be thankful that the formula's worked and that he's asleep again." And since he seemed contented for now, Elizabeth felt safe leaving him temporarily. She went and turned up the thermostat and changed into a clean white turtleneck.

Back in the living room once again, she sank into the armchair, wanting nothing more than to let the waves of tiredness wash over her. But instead, she reached for the phone. She had to call Jenny; she owed it to her.

"How are you? *Where* are you? What did you decide about the baby?"

Elizabeth couldn't help smiling at Jenny's rapid-fire questions. "I'm beyond tired and sinking fast. I'm home. And the baby's right here beside me."

"I'm so glad."

"I named him Ritchie, after Rick."

"So how does it feel having Ritchie home?"

"He's only here temporarily," Elizabeth blurted out. "I— I'm keeping him while Travis gets straight on his fathering techniques."

"You've lost me somewhere."

"Travis is going to adopt the baby."

Jenny sat back in her kitchen chair, staring in stunned amazement at the telephone in her hand, almost more shocked than she'd been at Elizabeth's original idea of giving up the baby without seeing him. "Let me get this straight. You're keeping the child temporarily, until Travis proves himself, and then bye-bye?"

"We both agreed on it."

Jenny bit her lip to keep from saying, "You're both nuts!" Aloud, she said, "Don't you think you're setting yourself up for heartache? What if you can't give the baby up when the time comes?"

"As I told you in the hospital, I know nothing about this mothering stuff. The baby will probably be relieved. Just a few minutes ago, he was screaming at the top of his lungs. I couldn't believe someone so small could make so much noise. Oh, Jen, I felt like an axe murderer."

"What crime did you commit?"

"I took him out of his bunting."

"That's a felony if I ever heard one, for sure. Let's translate here. You woke him up. He was probably startled, so he cried.

That's how babies let you know they're a trifle put out, or hungry, of just feeling yucky."

"Or wet. Or worse."

"See, you're catching on. How did you get him to stop crying? I don't hear any sound effects in the background."

"I bribed him with a bottle."

"Good for you. You're learning. You've got good natural instincts, trust me on this."

"Really?"

"Yes, really. By the way, when you feel you need a break from the baby, my niece Louisa is a terrific sitter. She lives about a half mile from you and she can use her parents' car, so you wouldn't have to worry about picking her up and taking her home. You can even call her on short notice if you just have to get out for an hour or two."

"I hadn't even considered what I'd do about Ritchie if I wanted to go out alone for a while."

"She baby-sat my youngest, Vince, when he was a newborn. She's seventeen, terrifically responsible, and saving for college. And Elizabeth—Louisa is a treasure. When you get more used to this 'mothering stuff,' as you call it, you'll learn pretty quickly that a good sitter is worth her weight in gold. Louisa's very much in demand. I wouldn't give her name to just anybody. Think about it."

Elizabeth reached for the pencil and scrap pad she kept near the phone. "Okay, what's the phone number of this paragon of a babysitter?" she asked, scribbling the number down as Jenny reeled it off.

"Okay, enough chatter for now, Elizabeth. I won't keep you. Having been around the block myself three times, I know you're tired. Do you have what you need? Can I get you anything? Do you feel all right about being alone with Ritchie? Do you want some company?"

"Travis went out to do some shopping. I'm sure I'll be fine. But thanks, anyway."

"In that case, Brad and I'll pop over tomorrow sometime in the early afternoon to see how you're getting along."

"You don't have to. I know how busy you both are."

"We *want* to. Besides, Vince is in day care, and Mark and Teddy are in elementary school, so we don't have to be home until about three-thirty. And Elizabeth, one last thing. I'm not trying to push my views on you, but please, don't try to decide too soon about whether or not to give up the baby. Give yourself some time. You need it. *Both* of you need it."

Shaking her head, Jenny hung up the phone. Having had three babies of her own, she didn't see how Elizabeth would ever be able to give up her baby once she allowed herself to become attached to it.

AS SHE WAITED for Travis to come back, Elizabeth expected the familiarity of her house to affect her as it usually did—to absorb her into itself. But for the first time, her surroundings failed her. She'd been gone three days; it seemed like three lifetimes. She closed her eyes, envisioning what it would feel like to sleep in her own bed, surrounded by the things she'd assembled over time.

Maybe being home would help her regain her emotional balance and she could find her way back to normalcy, she thought with a feeling of desperation. She hadn't expected to be caring for the baby; she'd thought she'd be back at work after a few weeks, with minimal responsibilities. Things would be as they once were, she'd thought, her only worries the woodworking projects she'd had pending and the commissions she'd undertaken.

And now it appeared that she had taken on, at least temporarily, the biggest project in her life: Ritchie. She looked down at the child sleeping so contentedly at her feet and feared that things would never be the same again.

6

As HE ENTERED the supermarket, Travis knew a moment of almost complete panic at having to shop. Since he was on the road most of the time, he ate out, hardly ever shopping for himself, at least not extensively. And when he did eat at home, the menu usually consisted of frozen TV dinners. Occasionally he went so far as to grill a steak. But he'd never, ever attempted to shop for a baby.

After making his way through a mine field of fresh produce and canned goods, Travis zeroed in on the aisle marked Baby Supplies. Disposable diapers were stacked according to the weight, age and sex of the baby. Cases of formula were similarly arranged, and displayed according to content: iron, iron-free, milk, milk-free, powdered, liquid, ready-to-use, with and without bottle. The choices were endless. Fortunately, he had the name and kind of formula the hospital pediatrician had recommended.

He started with diapers, then added formula, bottles, lotions, cotton balls, Baby Wipes, the bottle warmer Elizabeth had mentioned; he hoped it was the right kind. One thing led to another and before he knew it, the cart was almost too heavy to push, the items stacked so high he could barely see over them. And just when he thought there was nothing else to buy, he spied a display of stuffed animals, and promptly lost his heart to a soft, pink pig.

And after all the baby things had been taken care of, he stood in the main aisle, musing. The child would be taken care of. What about the mother? What did she have at home for herself?

He got another cart, then retraced his steps through the store, buying groceries. Milk. Fruit and vegetables. Chicken. He didn't know what she liked; he simply operated on automatic pilot.

The supermarket checker stared at him from the other side of the conveyor belt. "Triplets, sir?"

He glanced at the mountain of diaper boxes in the cart. "Er—no. Just one."

"Your first?"

Explanations defied him. "Yes."

SHE WAS SITTING in the chair, the baby asleep in the car seat. When she heard the door open, she was startled. Then stupefaction set in. "What—what *is* all that?"

She was staring up at him wide-eyed, as if she were in shock. "I'll be right back, Elizabeth."

"You mean—there's more?"

"Mmm," he murmured, disappearing out the door. "Back in a minute."

"Oh my goodness," she uttered in muffled tones.

Before Travis's arrival, she'd been sitting in the house feeling whipped. Depressed. Not to mention feeling totally panicked at being left alone with the baby. Now, just watching him take three trips to lug in the stuff he'd bought somehow appealed to her sense of the ridiculous, and lifted her spirits in spite of everything.

The look on his face was priceless. The poor guy looked almost dazed, as if all those packages had materialized by magic. Supermarkets probably declared holidays when Travis Logan came within buying distance.

One look at Elizabeth told Travis all he needed to know. Oh, man, he groaned inwardly, feeling like an abject fool. "Here I am, loaded down like a banana boat. You think I'm crazy, don't you?" he asked dispiritedly as he closed the front door and gazed down at the mountain of boxes and brown bags. "Elizabeth?"

If she wasn't extremely careful, she could very easily trample his feelings into the dust. Crazy? Extravagant. Generous. Impulsive. A soft touch. But crazy? "No, of course I don't think you're crazy." *Go on, Elizabeth, you're on a roll. Get yourself out of this one.* "Travis—"

"I didn't realize how much stuff I'd got until I saw people staring, and—oh, hell!"

She grabbed at his hand, trying to erase the pain of his embarrassment. "I never get a chance to do much shopping," she said quickly. "And of course, I can't drive for the next two weeks, and the chain stores don't deliver."

"You don't think I went . . . overboard?"

"Of course not," she said, smiling as she lied through her teeth. "I'd have done exactly the same thing."

"You would?" he asked, his voice tinged with doubt.

"Sure," she replied instantly, warming to her subject. "It's much easier and more efficient to buy in bulk. I know people who plan ahead for weeks to do massive coupon runs. I'll just put the stuff away." The question was, *where?*

"Stay put. Just tell me where things go and I'll do it."

"Okay. You do the lifting and fetching, and I'll supervise," she suggested with a smile.

They went into the kitchen and she showed him where to put everything, disappearing at least twice during the "stowing away" process to check on the baby. For his part, Travis followed directions good-naturedly, even helping Elizabeth to cover the bathroom vanity with a thick bath sheet, so there would be a place to change the baby.

"I meant to ask, how did things go with Ritchie while I was out?"

She sent him a wan smile. "He had his first screaming fit. We survived."

"Sounds like I had a lucky escape, huh?"

"I'm sure your turn's coming up fast, Travis."

"I'm shaking in my boots," he said.

"How much do I owe you for the items from the super-market?" she asked when they'd finished arranging things in the bathroom and were back in the kitchen.

"Get real," he laughed.

She blinked.

"You'd have to pay me a lot more money than you have to expose myself to that kind of torture," he said, entertaining her with a droll recital of his adventures in the supermarket. "Think of the stuff as a welcome-home gift. A kind of a—a baby shower."

"A baby shower."

"Elizabeth, what did I say?" He could see that she was shaking, that her hands were grasping the chair so tightly that her knuckles were white. "Tell me what's wrong," he pleaded.

"Nothing," she said as she drew a shuddering breath. "I just—when I have too much time to think, I start to think too much." She shook her head. "I'm sorry. I'm babbling, aren't I? Well, since you provided everything, I'll fix dinner."

She wasn't babbling, he realized. But he could tell that she was nearing the end of her emotional tether.

"You will *not* fix dinner," he informed her emphatically as he went to the refrigerator to retrieve the delicatessen and salads he'd picked up after leaving the supermarket. "You will sit. You can supervise and talk to me while I fix dinner."

"Who appointed you emperor?" she muttered. And then she heard Ritchie's cry, which sounded as if it threatened to turn into a full-throated wail.

"It appears that dinner's been postponed, at least tempo-rarily," Elizabeth said as she headed immediately for the living room.

"What do you think is wrong with him?" Travis asked, following on her heels.

"I don't know what's wrong with him, but I hope it's not as serious as it sounds."

"Let me get him for you," Travis offered, reaching down to unbuckle the safety strap of the baby seat. He couldn't help noticing how Elizabeth hovered. He said nothing when her fingers brushed his as he carefully lifted the squirming, crying baby into his arms.

"I think this would be a good time to try out the new changing table," she said as she headed for the bathroom. "I'm pretty sure we're going to need it."

"Do you think he's wet?" Travis asked, following in her wake.

"Or something," she muttered as she watched Travis lay Ritchie on the thick toweling that had been prepared. "You don't have to do this, you know."

"Hey, sooner or later I'll have to get down to business, don't you think?"

"Yes, I guess so," she agreed with a shaky laugh.

Elizabeth stripped off Ritchie's wet diaper and wiped and powdered his little bottom, while Travis braced his large hand against the baby's side so that the child couldn't fall off the vanity. Then Elizabeth took out a clean diaper and slid it into position under Ritchie and let Travis fasten the tapes.

But even when the job was finished, Ritchie was still screaming.

"What's wrong with him, Elizabeth?" Travis asked, his voice raising to counteract Ritchie's howls.

"Well, he can't be—uh—messed. We already took care of that. How about hungry?" she suggested as she picked the baby up and headed slowly for the kitchen.

"When's he supposed to eat?"

"According to the nurses, every four hours, but who's counting? I fed him while you were out, as an apology for making him cry when I took him out of the bunting."

"You mean he ate two hours ago and he's eating again now?" Travis asked.

"From what I understand, for the first few weeks, all they do is eat and sleep."

"Okay then, kid, it's dinnertime again."

"If you don't mind holding him, I'll get one of the ready-made bottles," Elizabeth said, her hand supporting the baby's bottom as Travis took the child from her.

"Uh, sure," Travis said, glad that she hadn't taken her hand away until Ritchie was securely in his arms. To his surprise, he wasn't as terrified as he'd been in the hospital room. Before he knew it, Elizabeth had the bottle ready and had sat down in the chair next to him. He put the child into her waiting arms.

To her embarrassment, Ritchie automatically began rooting for her breast through the thickness of her sweatshirt. She looked up, saw Travis looking down at her, an amazingly soft expression in his eyes. Wishing for a moment that Travis was still at the supermarket, Elizabeth turned her blush-warmed cheeks downward and quickly popped the bottle into the baby's mouth. "Don't you have anything to do?" she asked Travis pointedly.

"I can't think of anything that could eclipse this," he said softly, meaning every word of it.

"*Try,*" she begged. "Why don't you get the baby carrier and bring it in? It'll fit on the kitchen table easily. That way, we can have our dinner and not have to leave the room to check on Ritchie while we're eating."

"Okay, Elizabeth. While you're feeding the baby, I can put some of the deli out, how would that be?"

She wasn't hungry, not really, but she had a feeling Travis wouldn't eat if she didn't. "Sure, I could go for some food."

"It won't take me long."

"Take your time," Elizabeth said absently, virtually lost in thought as she held the bottle to Ritchie's mouth, watching him eat. Her breasts throbbed as if he were suckling from her own nipple rather than the bottle's. Experiencing an intense yearning from deep within, she almost wished she had decided to nurse—and then remembered why she hadn't—and felt the tears start again.

"Elizabeth, are you all right?"

"Yes, why?" she asked, trying to blink away the incipient tears as she looked up at Travis.

"Because the bottle's half-empty, but Ritchie's nodding off in your arms, and you looked kind of—breakable."

She glanced down and saw that Travis was right: Ritchie was practically asleep. To her amazement, she realized that she wouldn't have minded sitting there all day like that, with the warmth of his little body nestled against her body. "I'm fine," she said, determined to force her attention back to reality. *Her* reality.

"Would you like me to take over?"

"Sure, but he has to be burped," she said, transferring Ritchie to Travis's arms. "But not yet!" she warned as she picked up the dish towel she'd prepared for herself and draped it over Travis's shoulder. "*Now* you can burp him."

Travis put Ritchie to his shoulder, gently patting the infant's back until success was achieved. Once Ritchie was settled in his seat, Travis announced that dinner was served. "And Elizabeth—"

She looked up, startled, as his hand briefly kneaded the back of her neck. "What is it, Travis?"

"Let's try to forget for a little while, huh? Just pretend we're two people having a normal dinner."

"I don't—I don't know if I can," she said, Ritchie's presence making Travis's request virtually impossible.

"*Please*."

She drew a shaky breath. "I'll try," she said, not daring to admit that the shared supper was disturbingly similar to a cozy husband-wife reunion. "Tell me about your work,

Travis. I remember Rick—" She cleared her throat. "I remember Rick saying, 'My baby brother's really setting the computer world on fire.'" To her surprise, a trace of redness appeared on Travis's cheeks.

"I'm a partner in a computer consulting firm," he told her. "When a company has a problem, we analyze it and recommend solutions. Each of us has a different specialty. Mine is the mainframe, and since mainframe solutions are generally worked on at the site, I end up on the road a lot of the time. My partners, Kevin Riley and Jack Balzano, are both married. Since I'm single, and they have growing families, I get to do the traveling. It just kind of evolved that way."

"What kind of businesses use your service?" she asked.

"Any company that doesn't have a computer programming staff of its own. Banks, car leasing companies. We've also worked for large firms that do have computer staff but the programmers may have encountered a problem that stumped them. We come on-site, meet with management and data entry people, and then we customize a product to suit an individual company's needs. We make sure the product keeps working, and then we leave. And now that you know everything about me," he said with a wry smile, "tell me about woodworking."

"Well, my job is much more sedentary than yours. I create all kinds of objects, some decorative, some functional, out of different kinds of wood."

"How did you get into woodworking?"

"I guess you could say I learned at my grandfather's workbench. I spent summers at his farm in Rochester until I was ten. His workshop was in a converted barn. All I ever wanted to be was a woodworker. After high school, I studied design. It's through my woodworking that I met Rick and Kathy," she said shakily.

"Elizabeth, can you tell me why you decided to become a surrogate mother?" he asked, his voice gentle as he verbalized the unspoken question that had been simmering between them for the better part of two days.

"It's a long story, Travis."

"I've got the time if you have," he said, moving from the chair across from Elizabeth to the one next to her. "I can't get over the fact that you carried a child for someone else without even trying to make a profit on it, like everyone else who becomes a surrogate seems to do."

"Not everyone tries to profit from the childlessness of certain couples," she replied sharply. "I know of cases in which a sister, a friend, even a mother, have served as surrogates—with no monetary compensation. Of course," she said with what she hoped was a nonchalant shrug, "not everybody approves of what I did, even though I didn't do it for money."

Hearing the veiled bitterness in her voice, Travis recalled Elizabeth's reply when he'd asked her about family the day she'd gone into labor. "You're talking about your mother, aren't you?" he asked gently. "I remember your telling me that she didn't approve of your pregnancy."

"She certainly made her views on surrogacy abundantly clear. She thought I was crazy. She became pregnant with me by accident—she'd told me that more than once. The thought that *I* would become pregnant—'destroy my body' as she put it—for strangers really blew her mind."

"Well, I still think you're a special lady."

"Rick and Kathy were pretty special, too," she replied with a catch in her voice. "I didn't know anyone at all when I moved down to Baltimore from Rochester. I had no family other than my mother. And no other relatives at all nearby.

"For whatever reasons, I don't make friends easily. Maybe Baltimore's a hard place to meet people. I figured that since I didn't grow up here, I didn't know the 'in' crowd. Or maybe I'm just too much of a loner. Woodworking is a pretty solitary craft. Since I'm not a terribly social creature, my friends are usually other craftspersons I've met. I see them, but on a business rather than a personal level. Brad and Jenny are exceptions to that.

"I was exhibiting at a major regional craft show when I met Kathy. She bought several of my pieces. It was soon after she'd miscarried the first time. She and I became friends, and then I became friends with Rick, too. They didn't mind when I didn't bring a date." She flushed, biting her lip at what she'd revealed.

Travis was careful to say nothing at her startling remark. He wondered why she didn't date, though.

"As the three of us got closer, I saw how Rick and Kathy had to contend with so many false hopes. They put themselves through all kinds of hoops—medical, legal, the adoption networking system, all in their attempts to find a child.

"There was agony in Kathy's eyes every time she'd see a baby. I'd seen their pain, wept with them over miscarriages, felt their mutual agony at the hope of family denied. I couldn't stand it. Finally, I got the idea to be a surrogate."

"It was *your* idea? I was wondering how Rick and Kathy chose you to be their surrogate. I never realized that *you* chose *them*."

She nodded. "I sounded out Rick first. When he didn't think I was totally crazy, we decided to talk to Kathy. If our idea was going to hurt her, our efforts wouldn't be any good. We talked to her together. And then we cried together. After that, the tests started. Visits to doctors. And more false hopes—until the artificial insemination finally worked, and I became pregnant."

"And now—" He raked a shaky hand through his hair, but knew that he had to ask the question. He had to know. "Are you sorry, Elizabeth? Are you sorry you did this, took the medical and emotional risks, and now you find yourself taking care of a child you'd never planned to raise?"

"Sorry?" She stared at him, shaking her had. "No . . . oh, no," she whispered. "That would mean that the last nine months were a waste, that they should never have been. You weren't here, Travis." She didn't see him wince at her words. "You didn't see the joy they felt.

"All three of us shared in the pregnancy. We read books, but I concentrated mostly on the 'pregnancy' chapters and Rick and Kathy focused on the sections that started out, 'Now that your baby is born . . .' I didn't pay much attention to the how-to-be-a-mommy stuff. I didn't think I needed to. That was Kathy's role. Besides, if I'd stepped in, or stayed on the scene after the baby was born, Kathy wouldn't have been able to bond properly with the baby.

"And through all of this, Kathy was so terrific, Travis. She helped me cope with all the changes and stages of pregnancy. She and Rick were going to be my delivery room coaches. He painted and papered the nursery. Kathy and I shopped for baby clothes. I made a wooden mobile for the baby's room. I was just finishing a rattle—I'm sorry. I'm rambling."

"No, it's all right," he said, lightly stroking her arm. "Go on, Elizabeth."

"Afterward, I was going to be an honorary aunt. I was going to be part of a real family for the first time in a long time. All those plans, Travis. With all the planning we did— we never planned on this." She took a deep breath in a futile effort to suppress the awful loneliness. "Maybe I was selfish, maybe I wanted it too much."

"I honestly don't think you'd know *how* to be selfish." His words brought a fleeting smile to her lips.

"They would have made wonderful parents, wouldn't they, Travis?" Elizabeth asked brokenly.

"Yes, they would have," he agreed, not daring to ask why Elizabeth wasn't married, with kids of her own. Instead, he took her small, calloused hands in both his larger ones, hoping that somehow the strength of his touch would convey what words couldn't say.

"They were my best friends, Travis." The pain of the words was so terrible that she bent over, the tears streaming down her face.

Unable to abide her suffering any longer, Travis slid his arms carefully around Elizabeth, gathering her onto his lap. "What—"

"Shh. It's all right," he crooned, enclosing her in his warmth and vitality. He stroked her hair with one hand, while he wondered at the fact that he was deriving as much comfort from her presence as he was giving to her. . . .

Elizabeth sighed. His arms felt so good around her, lending her quiet support. For a brief moment, the past few days— the sorrow and the pain—all of it seemed to fade into the background. The only reality was the warm male strength that enclosed her.

The sudden cry of the baby shattered the quiet.

Stiffening, she backed away from him, suddenly embarrassed that he should always see her in times of weakness. She wiped her eyes with the backs of her hands. "I—I have to take care of Ritchie," she said, retreating in more ways than one.

With reluctance, he eased away from her. "I'll help you."

"You don't have to."

Travis assisted Elizabeth as she diapered and fed Ritchie once more. But instead of putting the child back in the carrier, she held him in her arms, a frown creasing her forehead. "What's wrong?" Travis asked.

"Some mother I'm turning out to be," she said, shaking her head in self-disgust. "I can't believe I haven't thought of this before. We don't have anywhere for Ritchie to sleep."

"Well, I didn't think of it, either, so don't go beating yourself up over it. If I'd thought of it, I could have brought some things over from the town house after I finished shopping at the supermarket. The crib was all set up, and there were some other things—"

She shook her head. "The crib would have had to be taken apart and even then, it wouldn't have fit into your car. You'd have had to use my van. It's still parked in front of the town house where I left it three days ago. Forget about the crib. It's too much trouble for now."

"You mean with all the stuff in the baby's room at the town house, there isn't something Ritchie could sleep in?"

"There's a bassinet," she admitted.

"A what?"

"It looks kind of like a long basket on legs, and has a white skirt around it. Ritchie can sleep in it until he gets a little bigger. There's a changing table, too. It's multicolored with a bolster around the sides."

"I could borrow your keys, drive over there, pick up the things we need, and drive back with everything in your van."

"No!"

"Is it that you don't want me to drive your van or that you don't want the things that Rick and Kathy prepared, Elizabeth?"

"No, to both questions. Of course you can use my van. And as for the things in the baby's room, I helped Kathy pick them out." She looked at Travis as he leaned against the kitchen counter, his arms folded across his chest. Surely he had to be just as exhausted and stressed out as she was, yet so far, he'd handled everything that had come his way without protest or complaint.

"Don't go out now, Travis. You look as tired as I feel." And, she admitted reluctantly to herself, she didn't want to be alone with the baby. Not this first night. Not even for the amount of time it would have taken Travis to go back to the house, disassemble the crib and bring it back. "You've had enough to contend with, what with your shopping expedition. It's late, and I'm sure we can manage."

"I'm glad you said 'we.' You hang on to Ritchie for a few minutes and I'll see what I can scare up in the way of a bed for him tonight."

Travis's cursory glance around the living room revealed nothing useful; neither did the kitchen, the small downstairs bathroom, or the small room with the daybed. When he came back into the living room, he saw Elizabeth glancing upward toward the stairs.

"Uh-uh, lady. No stairs for you. Doctor's orders."

"He didn't say no stairs. He said limited use of the stairs."

"Do you feel like walking up the stairs?" Travis asked patiently. "Be honest."

"All right," she grumbled, leaning back in the chair. "I'll wait."

At the top of the staircase was a hallway. To the right was a large bathroom with a claw-footed tub. To the left was a bedroom—Elizabeth's, he was certain. He scanned the room quickly. Finding nothing obvious, but coming up with the glimmer of an idea, he retraced his steps and made his way downstairs.

"You came down empty-handed, I see. I didn't think the upstairs would yield any possibilities. This is the end of the line, Travis."

"Not quite. Do you mind if I clear out one of your dresser drawers?"

She gaped at him. "What for?"

"The baby." He almost laughed at the wide-eyed amazement on her face. "We could line the drawer with a bunch of towels, kind of make Ritchie a nest, and put the drawer on the floor near the daybed."

She looked at the baby, then at Travis, then back again. "I think it might just work," she murmured. "Great idea."

Flushed with pride, Travis went upstairs again and took a drawer from Elizabeth's dresser. Intending to come back downstairs immediately, his pace slowed as he emptied the silky unmentionables onto the bed—and wondered how they would look on their owner. He wondered if he would ever know. . . .

Moments later, Elizabeth held Ritchie while Travis made up the drawer-bed with almost military precision. Then she put the baby down on his tummy, as the hospital nurse had suggested. Afterward, she tried to make desultory conversation, all the while desperately trying to smother her yawns. She struggled to stay awake, feeling as if she were wading through molasses. As she turned from the makeshift bed, she faltered; only Travis's quick action—and his arms around her—saved her from falling. "Thank you," she said gratefully.

He could see that she was wiped out, exhausted from the combined stress of the delivery and the trauma of grief. Her skin was almost translucent. Recalling the doctor's words, he realized that she was trying to tough it out. "You're out on your feet, Elizabeth. Why don't you get some sleep? I'll spell you. I'm not leaving. If it's all right with you, I'd like to stay over. You're so exhausted, once you fall asleep, you might not hear the baby."

"Travis," she said with a smile she was almost too tired to dredge up, "you've heard him scream when he's hungry."

"Right, I get the message," he replied with an answering grin.

"Right. Anyway, there's no way I could sleep through that, I promise you. But if you insist—"

"I do insist. I care about you, Elizabeth. I want to be here if you need me."

She was too tired to try to dismiss the fact that his words made her feel warm and tender inside. Instead, she carefully stored them away, forcing herself to deal with the problem at hand—a place for Travis to spend the night. "As a place for sleeping, the sofa isn't any great shakes. You could sleep upstairs in my bed."

"But then I wouldn't be close by if you or Ritchie needed me. I'll survive, Elizabeth, I promise you."

"All right. You'll find spare sheets, a blanket and towels in the linen closet that's at the top of the stairs. Take one of the pillows from my bed while you're up there."

"I'll do that. In the meantime, lie down for a while. Rest. Nap while he naps. I'll sit out here and relax on the sofa here with one eye open, just in case you don't hear when his 'nap' is over."

"That's not fair to you, Travis. You're just as stressed out as I am."

"*I* didn't have a baby," he reminded her gently.

"There is that, I suppose. But you helped."

They both laughed, aware of their attempts to "spare" each other.

It was the first time he'd heard her really laugh.

"Okay. I'll go lie down for a while."

Travis headed out of the room, then paused, turning around to face Elizabeth. "Don't close your door."

"Why?"

"*I* might not be able to hear if the baby cries. I sleep like a rock."

She knew he was right, but she couldn't prevent a shiver from playing havoc with her backbone.

When she didn't answer, he knew it must be because she was nervous about having a virtual stranger in such proximity. "Don't worry, Elizabeth. I don't intend to intrude. I won't come in unless it's necessary." And with that, he turned to leave the room.

"All right. Open-door policy."

After Travis went back into the living room, Elizabeth lay back on the daybed under the quilt, trying to figure out something that had been bothering her ever since she'd come home. She'd hoped that being back in familiar surroundings would make her feel better. Something was different, she realized.

At first, she put it down to the presence of the child, who was a constant reminder of the deaths of Rick and Kathy. But then she realized that it wasn't Ritchie who was causing her nerve endings to jump and her breathing to quicken. It was the presence of Travis Logan.

He was big, almost out of place in her carefully decorated environment. As she closed her eyes, she wondered what he thought of her corner of the world. And then she admitted to herself that she was relieved he had stayed—in case her exhaustion did prevent her from hearing Ritchie's cries....

TRAVIS FOUND a wool blanket and a pillow in Elizabeth's linen closet. Then he stripped off to his underwear and tried to make himself comfortable on Elizabeth's less than comfortable sofa.

Even though he was tired, he didn't fall asleep immediately. There were shelves of books around, but he didn't feel like reading. Instead, he lay back, letting his eyes explore the room.

The furnishings in Elizabeth's home in no way resembled the trendy modernism he'd seen at his brother's house—stainless steel and Plexiglas. This was a different reality.

He didn't know why, but the interior of the carriage house looked like Elizabeth, reflecting her own unique stamp. The furniture was homey, comforting, inviting. Colors and textures appealed to the senses. And above all, there was wood—wood everywhere.

A massive coffee table made of irregularly edged solid oak dominated the living room. The mantelpiece was filled with carved animals of some wood he couldn't identify, and a grouping of small rosewood boxes graced an end table, each piece different from the one next to it. Somehow he could sense Elizabeth's fine hand in everything around him. If he hadn't been so tired, he would have liked to examine each of the objects he was sure was the product of her woodworking skill. But his eyes were so heavy that even the bumpy sofa beneath him was starting to feel comfortable.

IT TOOK SOME TIME for the cries to register. At first, he thought the sounds were part of a dream. He'd done so much thinking about Ritchie that it wouldn't have been unusual to hear the cry in his dream. But then the cry came again, more insistently this time.

He jerked upright, throwing off the blanket and struggling into his jeans, then heading for the bedroom. A blurry-eyed glance at his watch told him it was just after 2:00 a.m. Elizabeth had told him to wake her, but he knew if he found her deeply asleep he wouldn't have the heart to do it.

As he made his way into her dimly lit room, he saw her already standing beside the dresser drawer. He could see the blurred outline of her body under the fine flannel gown she was wearing. "Sorry he woke you, Elizabeth."

"I wasn't sleeping very soundly, anyway. I'll take care of him, Travis. There's no need for both of us to be up."

"Exactly right. That's what *I'm* here for. *I'll* take care of him. You get horizontal. And no arguments, lady."

Elizabeth peered down at the squalling baby, then once again at Travis. "You're sure?" she asked uncertainly, too drained to even think about the way he was gently ordering her around.

"I've broken down and then reassembled computers that were about to be consigned to the trash heap. How difficult can it be to diaper and feed one small baby by myself? I'm sure I can handle it—I mean—him," Travis assured her.

"Thank you."

"Hey, it's all part of the service," he told her as he picked up the squirming child and headed toward the towel-covered vanity in the bathroom where all the baby supplies had been stored.

"Okay. It's just you and me, kid," Travis muttered, discovering that the child was sopping wet. Getting the diaper off was easy. *Now what?* he asked himself grimly, trying to remember what he and Elizabeth had done hours before.

Dry and wipe or wipe and dry? Then powder. How much to use? When he sneezed twice, he realized he might have used too much. And then there was the diapering itself. He would never have believed that *he* would have to handle a baby.

Thankfully, he told himself, there was no one to observe the all-thumbs clumsiness that had him ruin his first effort: he managed to stick the tape to the wrong part of the diaper. Despite the temporary setback, however, he refused to consider calling in reinforcements. Computer parts were smaller and more delicate than baby parts; of course he could survive diapering one tiny baby. Computers were certainly more dependable and less dangerous, he found, grumbling under his breath as he got sprayed from the neck down.

Ignoring the discomfort, Travis concentrated on the task at hand. But finally, the diaper was right side up and right side out, and he'd managed to make the flaps stick to the plastic band. "Thank God it doesn't need pins," he muttered fervently as he slipped the child into a dry nightshirt. "The poor kid would end up being a pincushion."

His hands still shaking with tension, Travis looked down at the child who was still crying plaintively, and realized that his job wasn't finished. Ritchie would have to be fed. Again. Another new experience, Travis told himself wryly as he quickly stripped off his wet T-shirt and hurriedly wiped himself off with a damp towel.

Picking up Ritchie carefully and holding him against his bare chest, Travis went to the kitchen. With a sigh of relief, he located the goody bag from the hospital, rummaging until he found what he was looking for.

"Thank goodness for the ready-made formula," he sighed. He wasn't sure he was ready to cope with the baby *and* the rigors of the bottle warmer. He sat down in the kitchen chair as Elizabeth had done, cradling the baby in the crook of his arm. . . .

ELIZABETH HAD TRIED to get back to sleep once Travis had walked out of the room with the baby in his arms. But even though she'd closed her eyes, sleep hadn't come. Instead, she'd listened—for what, she wasn't quite sure. Of course she trusted Travis with the baby, but she didn't know if he was really up to coping.

She was treated to a concert of baby cries and low-voiced masculine grumbles, but nothing that set off any built-in alarms. Eventually, she heard Travis leave the bathroom and head for the kitchen. . . .

AFTER RITCHIE HAD GUZZLED his bottle and burped a few times, Travis went back to Elizabeth's room and put the now-sleepy baby back in the drawer-bed. But instead of retreating to the living room, he followed some deep-rooted impulse and turned toward the bed.

"What's wrong?" Elizabeth whispered, her eyes following Travis's every movement as he came toward her.

"Nothing," he hastened to assure her, his voice pitched low in response as he sat down on the edge of the daybed. "Ritchie and I both survived my first solo effort at diapering and feeding, even though I got a little damp in the process. And I—" He swallowed, feeling foolish, wishing he'd had the strength to ignore the skittering flashes of tenderness and desire that had impelled him to Elizabeth's side. "I just wanted to check on you," he concluded huskily.

To her annoyance, her attention splintered—between the hair-whorled chest, the flat stomach with which she was practically at eye-level—and the warm, heavily-muscled thigh that pressed up against her hip. "I'm fine," she managed, wishing she could ignore the tremors of awareness that raced through her like wildfire in reaction to Travis's nearness. "Why don't you—get some sleep?" she urged, knowing that once he'd left the room, his effect on her would have to dissipate.

She held herself very still as he brushed her cheek with his knuckles, then eased off the bed. The mental image of the man taking care of her child soothed the ache in her heart, but another kind of ache kept her awake. . . . Every time she closed her eyes, he was with her, the rough texture of his voice echoing in the darkness, the tantalizing memory of his partially clad body edged behind her eyelids, and her flesh still tingling where his body had pressed against hers.

Aware of Travis as never before, Elizabeth wondered what it would have been like if the hand that had so briefly brushed her cheek had lingered—if his touch had gone from comforting caress to fiery passion? What if he hadn't walked out the door? Her attempt to ignore his nighttime visit kept her up into the wee hours of the morning, till she finally fell into an exhausted sleep.

SHE WOKE WITH A START, disoriented, her heart pounding. The room was bathed in sunshine. Bright morning light streamed through the slats of the miniblinds. The bedside clock showed 8:45 a.m. And all she heard was silence.

"Oh, no!" she thought, her heart beating frantically. "Ritchie should have been awake for a 6:00 a.m. feeding. Maybe he was sick, or—" She was afraid to even think the words that blazed across her frantic mind: maybe he wasn't even breathing! She practically leaped out of bed, ignoring the pain of her stitches and the fact that she almost tripped over the tangled bed sheets in her efforts to check on the baby.

Her mouth went dry as she stared down into the empty drawer-bed. The house was silent. And Ritchie wasn't there.

As she raced out of the bedroom, she risked a glance at the bathroom, noting the residue of powder and crumpled Baby Wipes on the vanity—the proof of Travis's adventures with the baby. She tore out of the bathroom thinking the unthinkable. Travis had wanted the baby desperately—maybe he had taken him.

Her frantic search ended in the living room, where she froze in astonishment. Pausing to collapse into an armchair, she saw that Ritchie was fine. They were *both* fine.

Ritchie was wearing a clean nightshirt and was safely strapped into the baby carrier, which was on the floor. And there, scrunched on her living-room sofa, his arm loosely grasping the edge of the carrier, was Travis. His hair was tousled, his head crooked into the hollow of his shoulder, his back angled against the corner of the sofa. His cheeks were shadowed by the overnight growth of beard, his firm, well-shaped mouth slightly parted.

Lying there asleep, without his glasses on, he looked so defenseless. But even at his most vulnerable, he was *dangerous*. To her. Looking down, she was startled to see her own hand, trembling—and outstretched toward him.

She backed away, shocked that whatever dangerous magnetism drew her to him was growing stronger each time she saw him. She was becoming dependent on his presence. Having him nearby somehow made her feel good. That in itself scared her. What would happen when he left to go back to his own life?

She recalled his endearing embarrassment after his shopping spree. And she remembered only too well his tenderness when he'd pulled her into his arms and onto his lap, as he'd tried to stave off the crushing weight of her grief. *Endearing?* Where had that come from? And *tenderness*. Was she beginning to care for him? No! It was out of the question. More than that, it was unacceptable. She knew better—had learned the lessons of the past all too well.

She was going to have to ask Travis to leave, she decided, as she went to the kitchen to brew the coffee. She was afraid of liking him too much, of becoming dependent on him, afraid of what he made her feel . . .

TRAVIS DIDN'T KNOW what woke him up—the smell of coffee, or the protest of cramped muscles as he tried to uncoil his body from its position on the sofa. He came to full awareness when Elizabeth's presence filtered through his sleep-drugged brain. "Sorry."

"For what?" she asked.

"I decided if I had him out here with me, maybe you'd get some sleep. I managed to stay up 'til 6:00 a.m. and fed him again, but then I guess I conked out. How's the kid?"

"He's fine. Well, he's asleep and quiet."

Travis got up in slow motion, so stiff from his night's "sleep" that he could almost feel his bones creak. "I feel like the Tin Woodman in the *Wizard of Oz*," he groaned.

"I can't offer you oil, but how about some fresh coffee?"

"I'd love some. I'll get it—"

"Uh-uh. My turn. I'm sorry you were so uncomfortable," she said moments later as they sat across from each other at the breakfast table, sipping coffee.

"I survived. I'm not so sure about my neck, though," he said as he gingerly rubbed the back of it. "But I wouldn't mind using your sofa again tonight," he said teasingly.

"Uh—I have to check on Ritchie."

His eyes narrowed at the way she left the room without replying. Moments later she was back, retrieving one of the last ready-to-use formula bottles. "How about if I feed him while you drink your coffee?"

"I can manage," she told him.

"Can I stay over tonight?" he asked again.

She shook her head.

"Why not, Elizabeth?" Things had gone so well the night before—why was she changing her mind now? "I want to help you."

She swallowed. "You have things to do. Maybe you can catch up on your business at the house—"

"There's nothing that urgent," he assured her. "And besides, the doctor said you'd need assistance of some kind."

Elizabeth didn't know Travis well enough to decide whether he was putting himself at her disposal because of some overdeveloped sense of responsibility, or simply because of doctor's orders. She simply knew that she found both ideas unacceptable. Furthermore, Travis was a strong, independent man with no ties. His involvement might be only an impulse—a whim. She had no way of knowing whether he would stick around if the chips were down.

"I can cope, Travis. I'll be fine. We'll both be fine."

"When you called me from the hospital the other night, you agreed—I didn't force you—you *agreed* to keep the baby for a little while, until I could get settled. And you agreed to give me a chance to prove to you that I can share taking care of him. How the hell am I supposed to demonstrate my so-called 'parenting ability' if I'm not here? By remote control? Or are you reneging on our agreement?"

"I'm not reneging on our agreement. I wouldn't do that. You can demonstrate your 'parenting ability' as much as you like. You don't have to do it twenty-four hours a day. You can come—during the day, see Ritchie whenever you want." Travis's staying the night smacked too much of playing house—Mommy and Daddy.

"I can get you a nurse, or a companion," he offered.

She steeled herself, telling herself that she would be better off going it alone. "No, I can handle it."

"Fine," he bit out, knowing that he couldn't force himself on her. Travis sensed that not only didn't she want him staying overnight—she didn't want him around at all. Period. She was certainly under no obligation to let him stay.

If ever a lady had signs saying Keep Out, she was the one. Travis saw how she managed to do just that, erecting what he'd come to think of as "the facade."

He did *not* want to go—either away from Elizabeth and the baby, or back to Rick and Kathy's empty house. Travis had to fight sickening waves of depression every time he walked through the door of the town house—where everything was cold no matter what the temperature was outside. But he couldn't tell Elizabeth that.

He'd discovered that he liked being needed—by Elizabeth. And by the tiny baby who had somehow already managed to become a part of his life. And more than that, dammit. Though he didn't know why, Elizabeth had become part of his life, and he didn't want to lose her.

But he didn't have *her*, he acknowledged wearily. All he really had was her promise to eventually let him adopt the baby. That was something, but certainly not all he wanted.

He squared his shoulders, knowing there was no choice. He had to leave.

"Space. You need space, Elizabeth. Well, maybe *I* need space, too," he said in an undertone, getting abruptly to his feet. "Fine. You've got it."

"Where are you going?"

"Back to the house."

"You're leaving now?"

"Yeah."

"Don't you want any more coffee?"

He tried to ignore the fragrant aroma that was intoxicating his senses. Sometimes, self-preservation outweighed even the need for a second cup of coffee. "I'll pass. Like you said, I've got work to do in the house. If you want anything, just give me a call."

7

WORK. Travis had told Elizabeth he had work to do in Rick and Kathy's town house. He shuddered, hating the oppressive, almost claustrophobic atmosphere that threatened to smother him every time he came back to this place. Even the damned plants were dead. Determined to conquer his feelings of dread and depression, he made himself a second cup of coffee from a jar of instant he found in the refrigerator. Then he phoned his office in Connecticut and talked to Leah Rabinowitz, the office manager.

"Just checking in, Leah. Any messages?" he asked, determined to force himself into a semblance of his normal business routine.

"We've got a possible new retail client in Petersburg, Virginia, and a sporting goods chain that's headquartered in Tarreytown, New York. And Blackwood and Wells, in Denver, want to talk to you about upgrading their system," Leah added.

Travis scribbled down what she was saying, shaking his head when she got to the Blackwood and Wells account. "I told them when I looked at their business patterns over the last five years that the system they had wasn't going to work for long. They didn't believe me."

"And now you can tell them 'I told you so,'" Leah said tartly.

"Yeah, right. That's definitely the way to attract clients. No, I'll work up the specs for an upgrade when I get back to Connecticut—and take out my 'I told you so's' in the fee we'll charge. Thanks for the messages. But I probably won't be able to solve our clients' problems without access to the on-line system that's sitting up in Connecticut. Anything else?"

"Not right now. Well—everyone wanted to know how you're doing down there in Baltimore. And when you're coming back."

"It's not as straightforward as I thought it would be. Originally, I thought I'd just have to execute Rick's and Kathy's wills and that would be all. But—well—it's going to take more time than I thought."

"More details than you expected?"

"Yeah, I guess you could say that." Elizabeth and his brother's son were definitely unexpected "details," he told himself wryly. "Thanks again for the messages. And say hi to everybody in the office for me."

"Will do, Travis. Take care."

Travis was glad he had to make some business calls. He couldn't do much for his clients except touch base. But at least the resultant conversations helped to counter the oppressive stillness of the town house. Then, unable to put off his rendezvous with the rest of the place any longer, he went upstairs to shower, shave and change clothes.

The shave made him feel more human; the hot shower helped to work out the kinks of the night before. But even the pulsating jets of water couldn't melt the ice that penetrated his bones. And turning up the thermostat did nothing to dissipate the inner chill generated by the yearning emptiness of the nursery. He wasn't prepared to handle the task that had been at the back of his mind for a while now: moving some of the items in the nursery to Elizabeth's carriage house.

With ever-slowing steps, he approached the brightly decorated room.

Later. He could do it later. It didn't have to be done now. After all Elizabeth didn't know he planned to do it. She hadn't asked him to do it. Hell, she'd barely asked him for anything.

With a massive effort, he steeled himself to cross the threshold of the room that had been meant to celebrate the beginning of life. Blanking out his mind as much as possible, he decided to take the white-skirted bassinet, the multicolored changing table with the drawers underneath, and whatever else was easily portable and could fit into his car.

As Elizabeth had said, the crib would have to be broken down, and he simply didn't feel like asking her for the keys to her van. He also left the rocking chair for another time.

Just before leaving, he went back for a stack of books on babycare he'd noticed on a shelf, and the wooden mobile which he now realized Elizabeth must have made herself.

WHEN THE DOORBELL RANG, Elizabeth thought Travis had come back. Instead, she found Brad and Jenny Fairhall on her doorstep, each of them holding a brightly wrapped package.

"How are you holding up?" Brad Fairhall asked softly as he set his package on the coffee table and gave Elizabeth a hug.

"I'm—hanging in there, I guess you could say," she replied as she briefly returned Brad's bear hug. "Jenny's been great, coming to the hospital, listening to me complain over the telephone."

"Hey, visiting you is no hardship, Elizabeth. Neither is giving you some support over the telephone. That's what friends are for, you know," she said, putting her own package on the sofa next to Elizabeth. "How's the little one today?"

"Fed and changed just before you came."

"No crises? No more taking off his bunting and then thinking you're guilty of child abuse?" Jenny asked with a teasing grin, noting with satisfaction how much better Elizabeth looked and sounded today, compared to a few days ago.

Brad cleared his throat. "Jenny, my love, I remember you as a new mom. You were even worse. You want me to tell tales out of school?"

"Enough, Brad!" Jenny cut in hastily. "If Ritchie's awake, Elizabeth, why don't we bring him out so he can see you open his presents?"

"Yes, Ritchie can come out," Elizabeth said, shaking her head at the lively banter that didn't mask Brad and Jenny's loving relationship.

Elizabeth went into the bedroom and lifted the still-awake Ritchie out of the drawer-bed, wrapping him lightly in a blanket.

Jenny said nothing as she noticed the easy way Elizabeth carried the baby—a far cry from the panic-stricken woman in the hospital. "He's looking really good, Elizabeth."

"Hi, little guy," Brad said softly as Elizabeth sat down on the sofa with the baby.

"Why don't I hold Ritchie while you open the packages?" Jenny offered.

"Okay. Ritchie, this is Aunt Jenny," Elizabeth said.

"That's right, honey," Jenny cooed softly, noticing how Elizabeth hovered for a moment, her hands lingering on Ritchie, hesitating, before carefully handing the baby into Jenny's waiting arms. Jenny had to hide a smile, knowing from her own experience that Elizabeth was behaving on pure instinct—making a kind of security check to reassure herself that her baby was okay. "And that big bear of a man over there is Uncle Brad. And now that the intros are out of the way, open the boxes."

"Open mine first," Jenny ordered when Elizabeth reached for the smaller one.

Amused by Jenny's childlike insistence, Elizabeth smiled, then fumbled awkwardly with the massive red bow on the first box. Inside was a mammoth, honey-colored teddy bear, which was exquisitely soft and squeezable.

"My two-year-old has one just like it," Jenny said. "It's so big, he used it as a cushion before he discovered it was really a toy."

"It's a wonderful bear," Elizabeth said huskily, leaning over to place Ritchie's tiny hand on the teddy bear's head.

"Now open the other one," Brad urged in his quiet way. "I'm feeling neglected."

The second package was smaller and heavier, and yielded a carved wooden music box, one of Brad's many specialties. This was the box she'd asked him to make for Rick and Kathy. It was to have been her present to them.

Her eyes flooded with tears as she carefully lifted the box out of its nest of packing material. On the lid and the sides were raised depictions of farm animals: a cow, a sheep, a horse, and more. And when she lifted the lid, she heard the familiar strains of "Old McDonald Had a Farm."

"Well, you wanted it to be finished in time for the little critter's birth, so I was hustling to get it done."

"Critter?" Elizabeth echoed, a ghost of a smile edging through the tears that came at the thought that Rick and Kathy would never see either of the gifts—or their son.

"That's what comes from having grown up on a farm," he replied, glad his clumsy attempt at humor had coaxed Elizabeth's mouth into a glimmer of a smile. "What do you think of it?"

"Oh, Brad, it's wonderful!" she exclaimed as she came around the coffee table and gave him a hug. In turn she was enveloped by the tall man with the shy, quiet manner.

WHEN TRAVIS got to Elizabeth's house, he used the key he'd borrowed from her the night before, before going shopping. When he opened the door, he felt as if he'd been punched in the guts. Elizabeth wasn't alone. Travis barely noticed the woman sitting on the couch. Instead his attention focused on the man with Elizabeth—obviously a man with whom she was on intimate terms, since he had his arms around her and she was raising no objections whatsoever.

Travis's mind replayed what Elizabeth had said two days earlier: "There is no man in my life." *Right*, he jeered inwardly.

"Sorry for the intrusion," he said, making his presence known. "Maybe I should come back later."

Elizabeth bristled at Travis's veiled sarcasm as she gently withdrew from Brad's arms. "You're not intruding, Travis."

"I just wanted to drop off some things from the nursery at Rick and Kathy's house," Travis said. "It won't take long."

"Never mind that, for now. I'd like you to meet Brad and Jenny Fairhall. I rent space in Brad's woodworking studio. Brad and Jenny—this is Travis Logan."

Brad Fairhall approached the other man, hand extended. "I'm really sorry about your brother and sister-in-law."

"We both feel your loss—yours and Elizabeth's—very deeply," Jenny added, rocking the baby gently in her arms.

Travis stepped forward to accept the handshake and the condolences. "Thank you. I appreciate the kind thoughts."

Elizabeth breathed a sigh of relief that the tense moment was over. "Brad brought over a music box he made for Ritchie."

Travis looked down and couldn't help but be impressed by the intricate carvings of baby animals that adorned the wooden box. "You do really fine work."

"Thanks," Brad said with a smile. "So does this lady here. Hope to see her back at her workbench soon."

"As soon as I can drive," Elizabeth said. "I wonder how Ritchie will react to the sound of a saw?"

"If he's anything like our kids, he'll love it. By the way, Travis, you mentioned you'd brought some things over in your car. Let me give you a hand with them," Brad offered.

"Thanks. I'd appreciate it."

As Elizabeth and Jenny sat on the sidelines and watched, the two men brought in the things Travis had raided from the nursery. He'd even brought the baby and parenting books that Rick and Kathy had read so faithfully. "Thank you for bringing all the things over, Travis."

"Sure. No problem. The stuff was just sitting over there. Why shouldn't the kid have the use of it all? I didn't bring the crib this trip."

"It'll transport better in my van. That's how Rick got it there in the first place," Elizabeth said, her thoughts turned inward with recollection.

"And besides, Ritchie looks so cute in his drawer," Jenny cut in, attempting to lighten the sadness she saw on Elizabeth's face.

At Elizabeth's direction, the men put the bassinet in her room, with the freestanding mobile suspended almost directly overhead. The changing table was placed in the bathroom, along with the baby clothes, and the books were put into a bookcase in the living room.

"Do you mind if I say hi to Ritchie?" Travis asked Elizabeth stiffly after the moving was done.

"Of course not. And then he can go back in the drawer until we fix up the bassinet."

"Hi, little guy," Travis crooned softly as he lifted the sleepy baby from Jenny's arms and held him against his chest. "Let's you and I have a little talk, huh?" Moving with slow, even steps, he took the baby back to Elizabeth's room.

"Travis seems very nice," Jenny said as she and Brad prepared to leave moments later.

"He is," Elizabeth agreed, deliberately saying nothing about her confrontation with Travis earlier in the day.

"Call us if you need anything," Brad said.

After the Fairhalls had left, Travis spent the better part of the afternoon at Elizabeth's house. He fed Ritchie once, changed him twice and knew a feeling of acute humility when the child fell asleep in his arms. And all the while he was there, he covertly watched Elizabeth, trying to figure her out, mystified as to why she didn't want him there, wondering why she found his presence so objectionable. He also tried to puzzle out his own gut-churning reaction to Elizabeth's easy familiarity with Brad and to the embrace he'd seen when first coming into her house.

He stayed as long as he dared, not leaving until just after sunset. Then, with a smothered sigh, he realized that he wasn't accomplishing anything constructive by intruding on Elizabeth. Bending over the drawer-bed, he gazed down one last time at the sleeping child. Then, before he could change his mind, he left the room and went to say goodbye to Elizabeth.

He pulled out his business card from his pocket and scribbled on the back of it before handing it to her.

She took it from him, staring at it blankly. LRB Associates, Computer Analysis/Systems Design. Stamford, Connecticut. "LRB?"

"Logan, Riley and Balzano. The office number is on the front of the card," Travis said. "My beeper number is on the back. It reaches me any time via a paging service. And the other number is the condo where I live in Connecticut."

"Why are you giving me this now?" she asked.

"I called in when I went back to the house this morning. I have to go back to my office. Things are happening, and all my equipment is up there. If I bring down some of the more portable stuff, I should be able to get some work done while I'm down here. I'll only be gone for a day or so."

She had no claim on him. He was probably only too glad to be getting back on the road. "It's all right."

"Do you want me to get somebody to come in and help you for a few hours, or even overnight?"

"That isn't necessary. I can manage. We'll be fine."

He winced at the flat tone of her voice. "Well, I'm not thrilled about leaving, myself. But when I came down here, I left a lot of things pending. I've got to do something about them. Once I get my own computer hookup, I'll be able to take care of things from Baltimore. In the meantime, I'll call you every day—to find out how Ritchie is."

"Okay."

Then Travis left.

The closing of the door signaled more than his leaving her house. Somehow the quiet sound seemed so *final*.

WHEN HE LEFT Elizabeth's house, it was nearly seven o'clock in the evening. Travis didn't stop at Rick and Kathy's place; he turned his car north and kept on driving. Stopping only for a bite to eat at a twenty-four-hour rest stop on the New Jersey Turnpike, he was walking through the lobby of his high-rise condo in Connecticut some six hours later.

Except for his colleagues at LRB, he didn't really know anyone in the bedroom community of moderate to upper-income homes and condominiums, which was a sprawling suburb of the New York megalopolis. His isolation was no one's fault but his own, he acknowledged as he picked up his mail from the service desk. He was rarely in town long enough to meet anyone.

Once inside the condo, Travis was able to give in to the day's emotional and physical stress, which had more than taken its toll. Drowning in fatigue, he dropped the mail onto the coffee table. He practically stumbled toward the bedroom, stripping off his clothes as he went. The only thing on his mind was sleep.

The next morning, he showered, donned slacks and a sweater and drove to Hamilton Square Industrial Park, where his office was located. To his surprise, Leah Rabinowitz came out from behind her desk and gave him a hug. Not used to such familiarity from her, he returned it clumsily.

"Travis, you're back! We missed you."

"I'm hardly ever here, Leah," he said with some chagrin, finding, to his surprise, that he'd missed them, too.

"Yes, I know you're usually out of the office. But not—not for a reason like this one. We're all so sorry."

"Thanks," he managed, giving her shoulder an awkward pat. "I appreciate it."

"Jack and Kevin are in their offices," Leah told Travis. "How about if I give you a while to settle in, then bring in the mail and systems reports?"

"That'll be great," Travis said as he headed for his private office. Once inside, he automatically turned on his computer, then sat down at his desk. In the center of the unlittered work space, he found an envelope. The card inside read: "With Deepest Sympathy," and had been signed by everyone in the firm.

Travis leaned back in his chair, his fingers smoothing over the clean lettering. He was touched—and ashamed. He hadn't given them credence, he realized—hadn't known they would care, at least not to this extent.

Through the course of the day, his colleagues drifted in one by one, offering awkward hellos and condolences, each subtly letting him know they cared.

He didn't get a lot of work done that first day back, but that didn't worry him. Reassured by the sense of routine, his ragged nerves were soothed by the familiar background noise of clacking keyboards and phone calls from clients who wanted it "yesterday." And most of all, he was warmed by the knowledge that he'd been missed.

To his amusement, Leah Rabinowitz watched over him like a mother hen.

"Lunchtime, Travis."

"You're a Jewish mother, Leah."

"I know," she said smugly. "It's an art that has to be carefully cultivated and practiced."

"And now you're practicing on me?"

"You look as if you need it. And *boychik*, with three children, and six and a half grandchildren, I think you could say that practice makes perfect. Now go take a break and eat some lunch. Jack and Kevin are waiting for you in the staff room."

Over lunch, Jack Balzano asked Travis how things were going in Baltimore.

"Things are more complicated than I thought they'd be." Travis took off his glasses and rubbed the bridge of his nose. "I have a problem, which means I may need to spend more time in Baltimore—a lot more time."

Jack's eyes narrowed, but he said nothing, waiting for Travis to continue.

"I discovered that I have a nephew," he said, not feeling sufficiently comfortable with his colleagues to mention the complicated circumstances of Ritchie's conception and birth and his own hope to eventually adopt the boy. "My brother had a son."

"Boy, you really do have a problem," Kevin said, shaking his head. "Take all the time you need. We can cover. Right Jack?" And at the other man's nod, he continued, "It's a good thing we hired that kid last month. He's young and hungry, a couple of years or so out of U.C. Berkeley, and good with mainframes. He can take over some of the traveling."

"It would certainly be one less worry, Kevin. The idea has my vote. What about you, Jack? It's up to you."

"I say go for it," Jack replied.

As Travis walked back to his office after the group lunch, he found himself forced to look at his colleagues in a new way. Jack Balzano and Kevin Riley were married; each had young children. "I couldn't relate to them before," Travis mused aloud. He wondered if it would be different now that there was a young child in his own life.

When Travis called Elizabeth later that night, he grimaced at the matter-of-fact tone of her voice. It told him nothing, but there was probably nothing to tell. He knew instinctively that she wouldn't lie about how Ritchie was; and if she was having any problems, she could count on Brad and Jenny.

"I'M MANAGING," Elizabeth had informed Travis when he'd called her the first night after his departure. "We're doing fine," she'd told him when he'd called the second night, deliberately making her voice even and unrevealing. And thanking the powers-that-be that there were no video telephones.

In fact Elizabeth was barely managing to keep up with the baby—but not much else. Her appetite had dwindled to nothing. She was tired to the point of exhaustion, and all her attention was concentrated on staying awake long enough to take care of Ritchie.

Perversely, she was angry with Travis for leaving and for staying away. And most of all, she missed having an adult to talk to. If Travis had been in town, she might have sunk her pride and called him. But since he wasn't, she would cope; she would have to.

After all, she reasoned tiredly, she'd struck a blow for independence in order to prove to herself and to Travis that she didn't need him, that she could succeed on her own. Well, she'd achieved her goal only too well. What right did she have to expect him to be at her beck and call?

The third morning after Travis's departure, the phone rang just as Elizabeth was trying to get ready for Ritchie's mid-morning feeding. Taking the bottle out of the warmer to cool, she picked up the phone on the fourth ring, all the while trying to hear what was being said above the sound of the baby's screaming.

"Elizabeth? I know I have the right number," Jenny said facetiously. "I can hear the baby in the background."

"Yes. It's me—I mean I." Her battle with grammar was interrupted by Ritchie, who was telling her in his own inimitable way, that he wanted food. *Now.* "Can I call you back, Jenny?" she asked as she gently cuddled the baby against her shoulder.

"Never mind calling. Brad's mother is watching the kids this afternoon. How about if I come over?"

"Sounds good to me," Elizabeth replied with a sigh before hanging up the phone and then devoting her full attention to Ritchie. After she finished feeding him, she put him down for a nap in the bassinet, then stood by the door to watch for Jenny. She didn't want the sound of the doorbell to wake Ritchie.

"How's the baby?" Jenny asked after giving Elizabeth a hug.

"He's fine," she said as she led the way through the living room and into her temporary bedroom.

"He looks good," Jenny said as she peered down at the snoozing occupant of the bassinet. And then her eyes narrowed as she looked back at Elizabeth. "He looks a lot better than you do."

"Thanks a lot," Elizabeth replied, leading the way over to the quilt-covered daybed.

"You look awful," Jenny said bluntly. "I thought you said Travis was helping you."

Elizabeth bit her lip. "He left, but he's not going to be gone long. And he's been calling once a day," she added in an attempt to convince Jenny.

"What do you mean, 'he left'?" Jenny asked. Her sharp eyes had missed nothing, including her friend's obvious strain and exhaustion. "Where did he go?"

"To Connecticut. On business."

"And when did he leave?"

"Three nights ago."

"And he's left you all alone all this time. That's certainly terrific. Just like that, huh? Well, I'm really impressed, I must say. So what if he calls you once a day? What can he do for you if he's in Connecticut! And *this* is the guy that wants to adopt Ritchie?" Jenny noted tartly. "He's here one day and leaving you holding the bag, so to speak the next? I take back what I said about him. He's not nice. If he couldn't—or wouldn't—stay himself, he should have at least had the decency to have arranged some outside temporary help for you."

"It wasn't like that, Jen. He offered to get me outside help. I told him no. And he did want to stay and help me. He didn't leave until I told him that I didn't want him here. I told him to go," Elizabeth admitted. She didn't add that she'd practically booted Travis out the door.

"*You told him to go,*" Jenny echoed, wondering at her friend's wisdom. "For heaven's sake, *why?* Why couldn't you have accepted the help the man was offering?" Jenny persisted in gentle tones. "Did he come on to you? Is that it? Is that why you don't want him around?"

"No!" Then Elizabeth thought of the times he had kissed her on the forehead. Held her hand. Wrapped his body around hers, infusing her with immeasurable comfort and tenderness. And, if she dared to be honest with herself, leaving her with yearnings for more of the same.

She didn't know what his behavior represented, but she definitely knew what it wasn't—a come-on. But she could hardly tell Jenny that as long as Travis wasn't underfoot, she, Elizabeth, wouldn't have to constantly worry about her reaction to him. "It wasn't anything like a 'come-on.'"

How could she have told Jenny the real truth—she feared that Travis's involvement with herself and the child might be an impulse on his part—a whim, considering what a strong, independent man he was. She couldn't bring herself to face the possibility that maybe he wouldn't be around when the chips were down.

"I told him I didn't need him," she said to Jenny. "I'm not some pathetic victim who needs her hand held. I'm used to handling things on my own. Other women do it."

But other women weren't emotionally shattered as well as physically drained, Jenny said to herself. "And how do you feel—*really?*"

Why bother to lie? Elizabeth asked herself dully. Her condition was obviously there for Jenny to see. "I feel like I'm asleep even when I'm awake. And I can't get any sleep because I can't seem to relax."

"Elizabeth, the first couple of weeks after giving birth is no time to be alone. Or to be too proud to ask for help. Your body has just gone through nine months of changes. Now it's going through a kind of physical and emotional withdrawal since you're no longer pregnant. It's perfectly natural that you should be tired and exhausted, not to mention depressed at being tired and exhausted, and you don't know how to pull out of it. On top of all that, you still haven't recovered from Rick's and Kathy's deaths, now have you?"

Elizabeth couldn't help staring at Jenny. "Are you psychic or what?"

"My dear, I've got three kids, and I've been through my own bouts of postpartum depression—especially after the doctor told me that Vince would be my last."

"Oh, Jen, I didn't know—"

"Hey, it's okay," Jenny said with a tremulous smile. "I've got my three little hellions and I'm thankful for them. Now, back to your problem. Let's get organized here. I haven't got a whole lot of time today, but I can certainly do some shopping for you, and take care of some of the things in the house."

"I've let everything in the house go to seed."

"Hey, you're taking care of the baby. Everything else *definitely* takes second place. And it just might be a good idea to give Louisa a call when she gets home from school at three-thirty this afternoon. She might be able to spell you in the evenings. That way, even if you have to walk the floor in the wee hours, you'll be walking it more rested. With the boys in school and day care, I can be here for a few hours tomorrow, too. So if you want, I'll stay and you can get out a bit."

"I don't want to get out," Elizabeth sighed wearily. "I just want a nap. One that lasts about a year might do it."

"Well, go lie down and grab one, then. But not one that lasts a year. And in the meantime, I'll call Louisa."

HER BUSY SCHEDULE notwithstanding, Jenny found time to pick up around Elizabeth's house, run some errands, and prepare a couple of meals. And Louisa came over to spell Elizabeth in the early evening. Their combined presence certainly helped, allowing Elizabeth some time to rest, even to snatch an occasional nap.

Elizabeth found that if someone else was present, she could turn off the instinct that woke her up every time Ritchie cried. The naps, short though they were, really helped. She awoke feeling amazingly refreshed.

But her helpers eventually went home. They weren't there when the dark, deadly quiet was rent by a crying child, when Elizabeth walked most of the night with that child in her arms, or when the terrible aloneness etched itself into Elizabeth's soul with the virulence of acid.

With every call she received from Travis, she'd hoped he would say that he was on his way back to Baltimore; she'd hoped he would renew his offer of help. If he had, she would have said yes like a shot. But his calls from Connecticut consisted of impersonal conversation—except when he asked about Ritchie. And since he didn't offer to come home, she couldn't bring herself to swallow her pride and ask....

"Be honest, Elizabeth," she told herself grimly the next morning, "you're so tired, you can barely manage to sterilize and warm Ritchie's bottles." Realizing how much she needed Travis, she finally conceded defeat, reaching for the telephone and calling his office.

"LRB Associates. Leah Rabinowitz speaking. May I help you?"

"I'd like to speak with Travis Logan, please."

"He's out of the office. May I ask who's calling?"

"It's all right, thank you. I'll—I'll call back later," she said, her response couched in perfunctory politeness. She wasn't even aware of hanging up the phone. *What would have been the point of leaving a message?* she asked herself, almost laughing at the sense of anticlimax. She'd finally admitted— to herself at least—that she needed Travis. And now he wasn't there. Well, it was her own fault, she thought cynically. She'd told him she didn't need him in the first place. But traveling was an integral part of the man's life. He might have left even if she *hadn't* told him to go. She was simply observing it at close range for the first time.

With a heavy sigh, she prepared to face another hellish night.

8

TRAVIS HAD FOUND HIMSELF enjoying his days in the office, even though in the past he'd always preferred to be on the road. To his surprise, he'd been invited to dinner at Kevin Riley's house. At first, he was ambivalent. He'd never really socialized with his colleagues before; but then, he'd never really been around them much, either. In the end, he'd accepted the invitation, much preferring the company of others to the solitude of his empty condo.

He had appreciated the good food and conversation. But more than that, he'd enjoyed watched Kevin's interaction with his two children, one a toddler, one an infant. Travis had caught himself wondering what Ritchie would be like in a year or two....

Now, after nearly five days in Connecticut, Travis secured his equipment for the trip back to Baltimore, his mind replaying his last encounter with Elizabeth. She'd told him that she didn't need his help, he reminded himself. Maybe her rejection was really a prelude to her changing her mind about letting him adopt Ritchie. His hands tightened reflexively on the steering wheel.

It was 8:00 a.m. and he was on his way back home to Baltimore. But where *was* home? he wondered bleakly as he entered Rick and Kathy's unheated town house. He flexed his shoulders, which were more than a little stiff from nearly seven hours of driving. Home wasn't the condo where he'd spent the better part of the last five days—where he felt like a stranger who was just passing through.

And home certainly wasn't Rick and Kathy's town house, which he intended to list with a real estate agent as soon as possible. Once again, he found himself hating its oppressive atmosphere. He hated rattling around in the emptiness that suffused him as if by osmosis. He felt as if he were an intruder in someone else's life.

Maybe *home* was a four-letter word that simply didn't belong in his vocabulary, Travis decided as he carefully transferred his computer and its peripherals from the car to Rick's study. It took him about an hour to get the system up and running to his satisfaction. And then because he couldn't put it off any longer, he reached for the phone, intending to call Elizabeth.

He replaced the receiver without punching in the numbers. "I've got a right to see Ritchie whenever I want," he muttered, picking up his coat once again. "Elizabeth said so." It was only when he was halfway to her house that he stopped to ask himself what he would do if she wasn't there. Where could she be? He could always call the Fairhalls, he reasoned; surely they would know....

Elizabeth jumped at the sound of the doorbell, praying that the noise wouldn't wake the baby. It couldn't be Jenny; she'd left at two-thirty, barely half an hour earlier. When she looked through the peephole, her heart started racing. By the time she'd unlocked the dead bolt and turned the doorknob, her palm was slippery with nervousness. The relief—no, the joy—she felt at his return scared her. She had to restrain herself from throwing her arms around his neck. "I thought you were still away."

"I just got back from Connecticut and thought I'd check in," Travis told Elizabeth, as if his showing up on her doorstep was the most natural thing in the world. "How's Ritchie?"

"Fine."

"Glad to hear it." Clearly his presence wasn't really necessary to Elizabeth. From the sound of her voice, everything was just aces. "And you, Elizabeth? How are *you?*"

The words hung in the air.

"Elizabeth?"

If she'd had any pride left, her answer would have been "fine." But suddenly, she couldn't seem to dredge up the effort to tell the lie. "I told you that I didn't need any help. Well, you were right, Travis," she said, ruthlessly suppressing the fear that she was leaving herself open for humiliation and rejection—the same kind of rejection she'd dished out to him. "I guess 'pride goeth before a fall.' I *do* need help."

She was leaning against the door frame as if she needed it to hold her up. Her hair was tied back with the inevitable ribbon, but today it seemed to droop as much as she did. She was wearing blue sweatpants and an oversize rugby shirt. And from the looks of her, she hadn't wasted much time eating or sleeping lately.

How much of it had been his own fault? He should never have left, should have forced her to accept outside help, since she hadn't wanted help from him. Wary of the way she'd rejected him before, he only said, "I'll call one of the agencies."

"Agencies?" she echoed.

"To get you some help."

She had to struggle to stem the onrush of weak tears. "I don't want someone from an agency, Travis. I—I just need—" She needed Travis. "I turned you down when you offered to stay overnight. I'm so used to being in control of my life, my work, everything—I thought I could do this on my own, too."

"No one can be in control all the time," Travis said as he slid an arm around her waist and gently urged her toward the living-room sofa. "Have you been alone here ever since I left?"

She shook her head. "Jenny came when she could, but with three young ones of her own, it wasn't easy for her and she couldn't stay very long. And her niece Louisa came after school and in the early evening. When they were here, I was able to relax a little. But once I was alone, I was on guard constantly. I tried to sleep with one eye open."

He framed her face between his hands, his thumbs gently tracing the shadows under her eyes. "It looks to me as though you've been sleeping with *both* eyes open."

"I couldn't help it. I couldn't relax unless I knew someone was there to watch Ritchie." She gritted her teeth, stifling her pride. "I was wrong. If you could see your way clear to staying for a few nights, maybe I could get a few hours of uninterrupted sleep."

Amazed at what she'd requested, he saw the tears shimmering in her eyes and knew that he was well and truly lost. "I'll spell you the next few nights."

She didn't bother suppressing her sigh of relief. "Thank you. I—oh, Travis, I—I just want things to go back to the way they were."

"Ah, honey, so do I," he murmured, drawing her into his arms.

"You can use my bed upstairs," she said, utterly bemused as the feel and smell of him swamped her senses. "It's got to be better than the living-room sofa."

"Now that's an offer that I wish I couldn't refuse," he said, recognizing the invitation for the olive branch it was. "But let's turn that around," he said, one arm drawing her closer still, while his other hand cupped her cheek. "You take a nap for a while, get your batteries recharged. I'll tell Ritchie all about my trip to Connecticut."

She flashed Travis a rueful grin. "That's tempting. But you must be tired from all that driving."

"I'm going to let that armchair of yours swallow me, you can believe that." He shifted his hands to her shoulders, gently turned her around, and gave her a light but firm nudge in the direction of her temporary bedroom. "Nap time," he said as he followed her through the doorway, then went over to the bassinet to say hello to Ritchie, whose eyes were open, even if they weren't focused on anything in particular.

"Hi, fella," Travis said softly, getting an approving glance from Elizabeth as he picked the baby up. "Let me tell you all about computers...."

Elizabeth was bewildered by the profusion of feelings that had descended on her with Travis's return. But right now, her mind was too tired to analyze all the implications. Later. She would worry about it later. In the meantime, her nap beckoned....

When Elizabeth opened her eyes again, it was nearly six-thirty in the evening. She stretched luxuriously, feeling amazingly refreshed. It could have been from the three hours and more of uninterrupted sleep. Or, if she were to be honest with herself, she would have to admit that her spirits were soaring simply because Travis was back.

"Feeling better?" Travis asked, looking up as Elizabeth came into the living room. Thankfully, she no longer looked fragile, shaken, so brittle that she might break.

"A hundred percent better," she said with a smile. "How did things go with the two of you?"

"We got reacquainted," Travis said, gently rocking the baby seat in which Ritchie was sleeping. "I'm going to be leaving for a while now, so I can get cleaned up. I'll be back in time for you to be able to get a good night's sleep."

"Would you like to come before that—for dinner?" she asked, a tentative note in her voice.

"I'd like that. What can I bring?"

"Nothing this time. Please? You're always talking about sharing, remember?"

"All right."

"Is there anything special you'd like?"

He was touched that as tired and stressed as she was, she would want to fix a meal for him. "Surprise me."

HE WAS SURPRISED. The woman who opened the door for him at eight o'clock that evening looked like a different person. Her hair had been tamed into a kind of knot, her face was gilded with a hint of blush, her mouth barely tinted with lip gloss. Darkened lashes framed her crystalline eyes. She was wearing a softly pleated print skirt topped by a turquoise sweater. He couldn't prevent his gaze from lingering at the way the wool outlined the lush fullness of her breasts.

"Is something wrong?" Elizabeth asked, wondering why Travis was staring at her.

He took a deep breath, his senses registering the fresh scent of baby powder and that of her more sophisticated perfume. "No. Nothing's wrong," he said as he crossed the threshold, handing her a bouquet of tulips and irises. "For you."

"I love spring flowers!" she exclaimed, her face lighting up. "Thank you. I'll just get a vase."

As she left the room, he caught sight of the table set with china, crystal, the tempting array of Chinese foods, and the fire burning brightly in the living-room fireplace. "You went to so much trouble," he called after her.

"I'm not really used to entertaining. I just sent out for Chinese."

"I love Chinese."

The meal was wonderful. The hot spiciness of *kung pao* chicken was balanced with sweet-and-sour shrimp and spring rolls. But more than by the wonderful food, Travis was affected by the care that had obviously gone into putting everything together. Heavy flatware gleamed on a wooden table that had been polished to a satin glow. As he glanced around the small dining area, he noticed more things made of wood—an intricately carved salt-and-pepper set, a wooden board with brass handles, a nest of wooden salad bowls.

"Elizabeth?"

"Hmm?" Holding her chopsticks aloft, she paused in the act of transferring a last shrimp from plate to mouth.

"These things made of wood—did you make them all?"

"Yes."

"Even the table?"

"Uh-huh. It was a studio project when I was studying with a master craftsman."

"How did you get it in here?" The table was so massive it looked immovable.

"Friends with strong backs."

"Do you ever wish you had a wood shop on the premises?"

"All the time. If I had a garage, or even a large basement, I'd be all set, but living here in this rented carriage house, I don't have access to either one. But I'm really fortunate since Brad has a terrific workshop out in the country and he lets me share it. That's where I do all my work."

"Wouldn't it be better to work at home?"

"Someday, maybe."

Travis saw the faraway expression on her face and wondered what she was seeing. "What do you mean by 'someday'?"

"When I sell enough to be able to afford the right tools and the work space to put them in."

After dinner, Travis cleared away the remnants of their dinner. "Are you ready for bed?" he asked when he'd finished and returned to the living room.

Elizabeth felt the warmth of a blush at his choice of words. "No, not just yet. I think I'll read for a while," she said, much preferring to sit and relax with Travis in the evening quiet. "If you want something to read, feel free to help yourself," she added, gesturing toward the bookcases.

He saw an assortment of novels, mysteries and a series of black leather volumes that turned out to be presentation binders. "What's in the binders?"

"My work."

"Sketches?"

"No. Photographs of actual work in progress, or finished projects."

"Do you mind if I have a look?"

"Of course not," she replied, pulling a volume off the shelf and handing it to him.

He sat down in one of the armchairs and leafed through page after page of Elizabeth's work—boxes and bowls, trays, chess sets . . . amazing that she could create such extraordinary beauty out of something as ordinary as wood. She was like her woods, he mused as he closed the volume and looked up at her—a rare combination of beauty, strength and delicacy.

She held her breath, anxious to hear what he thought of her work.

"This isn't woodworking."

She stiffened as hurt clawed at her insides. Why had she thought Travis would be any different? she wondered bleakly. Her usual response to this kind of blanket condemnation was to turn off mentally. Ignore it. Not this time, she vowed. Not ever again.

"How *dare* you," she ground out. "What do you know about it? Have you ever tried doing it? Do you know how long it takes to create these things? *Create.* It's not like painting by numbers, y'know. I'm tired of hearing people put down woodworking," she said as she snatched the binder away from him and stuffed it back onto the shelf beside the others.

"Whoa," he said, latching onto her wrist. "You want to tell me what this is all about?"

"I'm sorry. I guess I'm being too sensitive."

"Elizabeth, what did you think I was talking about?"

"That I spend my time *playing around* with wood."

"I never said that."

"No, you said what I did wasn't woodworking."

"What I should have said was, 'It's not *just* woodworking.' Elizabeth, it's art." Although she averted her head, he could see the bloom of color that tinted her cheeks. "Did someone criticize your work, Elizabeth?" he asked softly.

She stared down at her hands; his fingers were still linked to her wrist. "It's been known to happen. I'm sorry I over-reacted."

It was more than overreaction; he could see that. Politeness dictated that he should back off and change the subject. But caring overrode politeness. He couldn't back off, or change the subject, not without finding out what had happened to make her feel this way.

Releasing her wrist, he brushed his knuckles lightly across her cheek, gently grasping her chin with his fingers as she looked up at him. "Talk to me, Elizabeth. Tell me who or what put the shadows in your eyes."

She shivered at the tender note in his voice. "You'll think I'm a whiner."

"Somehow, I doubt that. I've never met anyone less likely to whine. I wish you were more likely to share, though. It doesn't feel good to be shut out."

She shook her head in wonder.

"You can't tell me?" he asked softly. "It's too painful?"

She shook her head again. "It's just—I guess I'm kind of programmed to keep it all to myself." She took a deep breath. "It's something I've heard all my life. My parents thought my 'messing around' with wood was ridiculous. When I signed up for drafting and wood shop instead of art and home economics in junior high school, they had conniption fits. When I was fifteen, they asked me what I wanted for Christmas— I told them I wanted a sander."

"And what did you get?"

"A sewing machine," she replied, her mouth turning down at the corners.

"Nobody ever gave you any support?"

"My granddaddy. See the animals on the mantelpiece?"

Travis had already seen them that first time in Elizabeth's house. There was a squirrel that looked as if it were ready to scale a bird feeder, a cat engaged in a well-mannered wash, a dog gnawing a bone. Each animal looked alive, poised for action. "I thought you'd done these."

"Oh, no. I don't have that kind of talent. Give me a block of wood and a carving tool, and all you'll end up with is a block of wood that looks like it's been nibbled. My granddaddy could make wood talk. When I was a little girl, he made the animals and a miniature chest of drawers, all with hand tools, no power tools. He let me watch while he was working. I guess that's where I got the idea of working with wood, myself. He was going to make me a dollhouse . . ." she said with a sigh, her voice trailing off.

"What happened?"

"He died when I was ten."

"But he left you a wonderful legacy."

"Yes." Then, "I'm going to make some tea. Do you want some?"

He saw her get up, squaring her shoulders, as if visibly pulling herself together. He didn't really want any tea. He was a coffee drinker by choice, but he could tell that she needed to be doing something. "Sure. Tea sounds fine."

He followed her into the kitchen, expecting a hot mug and a Flow-Thru tea bag. Instead, he saw her boil water, pour some of it into a flowered china teapot, then throw the water out. After putting loose tea into a little metal cage, she poured in hot water again over it into the china pot. Then she set out a pitcher of milk, a plate of lemon slices, and a bowl of sugar.

"I hope you like English Breakfast. I'm out of Earl Grey."

"Who?"

She had to smile at his blank expression. "They're different kinds of teas," she told him as she poured tea into delicate china cups, setting one in front of him. "I'm afraid I'm a bit of an addict. Have been ever since I met an English lady who introduced me to the joys of high tea."

"High tea?" he echoed, as he watched Elizabeth add milk to her tea. "We're talking itty-bitty sandwiches, huh?"

She sighed as she took a sip of the fragrant brew. "Oh, Travis. You're a philistine. We're talking sandwiches, breads, Scotch eggs, all kinds of scones with jams and Devon cream, berries . . ."

She was staring off into space, her gaze obviously focused on a faraway tearoom. "And where does one have high tea in Baltimore?" Travis asked.

"Oh, several of the hotels and restaurants do different kinds of teas. I haven't been in a while. Kathy and I used to have high tea in Fells Point on Wednesday afternoons." She set her cup down abruptly. "I think I'll go to bed now."

He set his own cup down and captured her wrist. "I'm sorry if I said the wrong thing."

She made no move to free her hand. Instead, she lay her fingers on top of the hand that held hers, squeezing gently. "You didn't. Don't feel you have to watch everything you say. And please don't feel you can't talk about Rick and Kathy. *I* intend to. I just—" She was winding down; she wanted nothing more than to go to sleep. "I just can't right now." She tugged on her hand. "Now, if you'll let me have this back, I'll clear away the tea things."

"You go get settled for the night. I'll take care of everything."

"Thanks."

He cleared away the remnants of their snack, his mind vaguely on the task at hand. A light film of sweat popped out on his forehead as he imagined the soapy washcloth trailing over her, her skin glistening, the water streaming over her...

"Keep your mind on the job," he ordered himself ruthlessly as he almost dropped a cup. He banked the fire for the night, making sure that the thermostat was set for a temperate seventy degrees Fahrenheit. He was about to get ready for bed himself. Instead, he headed for Elizabeth's room, intending to say good-night. When there was no answer to his soft knock, he pushed open the door. Ritchie was in his bassinet; Elizabeth was not in the room.

He found her sitting at the bottom of the staircase, looking up toward the second floor. "No," he said.

Her head snapped around. "No what?"

"Don't even think about it. And don't give me that innocent look. The doctor said limited use of the stairs."

She blinked, sending him a mulish look. "I've been doing it for several days now, in easy stages. Besides, I know lots of people who've never paid attention to that rule."

"I'm sure you do."

He was leaning against the wall, his arms crossed in front of his chest, his legs slightly spread. She hated the smug expression on his face. "You're not my keeper, Travis."

Why was she picking a fight, he wondered. If he rose to the bait, he knew he would put her on the defensive, and her claws would come out, like a cat. Then he heard her sigh. Instead of continuing to push her, he sank down on the step beside her. "What's so important up there, Elizabeth? I'll bring down whatever you want—clothes, shoes, linens—just say the word."

Conscience-stricken, she turned to him. "You can't bring it for me."

"Is it—er—unmentionable? I wouldn't look." To his amazement, she broke into a peal of laughter, which eventually dissolved into giggles that she tried to hide behind her hands.

"Sorry. What I want isn't portable. There's no way you could bring it down for me." She heaved a sigh. "I want a bath. I want to soak in my claw-footed tub until I closely resemble a grove of prunes. I thought since you were here, I wouldn't have to worry about Ritchie."

"A bath? That's what this is all about? *A bath?*"

For an answer, she glared at him. "You did ask."

"Finally, a problem I can solve." And without saying anything further, he eased off the step and scooped her up into his arms.

"What are you doing?" she gasped as she quickly linked her arms around his neck.

"What does it feel like?"

Heavenly, she answered inwardly, barely able to resist the urge to rest her head against his chest. "I must be heavy."

"No way are you heavy." He couldn't begin to tell her how good it felt to be holding her lush softness against him. "And I can't think of anything else I'd rather be doing," he said, tightening his arms slightly as he began to carry her very carefully up the stairs.

She liked the steady beat of his heart, felt the incredible warmth and security of his strong arms. She could almost feel her heart sink when the too-brief journey came to an end.

He set her gently on her feet, his hands palming her slender shoulders.

"Thank you."

"Now you can have all the bath time you want. Prune city, sweetheart."

Sweetheart. The endearment echoed in her head. Her thoughts were more than a little muddled as she absentmindedly gathered up a soft printed flannel gown and her teal blue robe and drifted down the hall to the bathroom.

Elizabeth ran the water full strength, then peeled off her clothes. Although the heat was on in the house, she shivered in the chill night air, and was only too glad to ease into the tub.

"Bliss," she murmured, leaning her head back against the cool porcelain as she sank beneath the surface of the heated, foaming water. No, it was more than bliss as the washcloth came in contact with still-tender parts of her body. This was sheer decadence....

But as she eased out of the tub, she was overcome by a wave of dizziness that sent her reeling. Bracing herself against the wall, she reached for the bath sheet that lay on top of the closed commode. She had barely finished wrapping the generous folds of thick terry around her when there was a rap on the bathroom door. "Wh-what is it?" she called.

He didn't like the slight hesitation in her voice. "Are you decent?"

Leaning against the cool tile wall behind her, she looked down at the towel she was clutching with one hand. "Yes, but why—" Before she could even get the words out, the door was opening, and she was watching him cross the threshold.

"I didn't like the way you sounded," he said, captivated at the sight of her towel-wrapped form against the backdrop of steam hazily emanating from the bathroom. "What's wrong?" he asked, drawing nearer.

"Nothing, really. When I got out of the tub, I felt kind of—woozy."

"Like your legs were made of cooked spaghetti, I'll bet. The water was probably too hot." Feeling a powerful surge of protectiveness, he tugged at her free hand. "Come sit down, Elizabeth," he urged.

Bemused, she yielded to the light pressure on her wrist as he gently tugged her toward the commode. "I'm fine now, Travis."

"Very fine," he echoed huskily. Her cheeks glowed, her hair was deliciously mussed. A pulse fluttered erratically in the hollow of her throat. And he felt his own pulse shift into high gear as his gaze was drawn past her smooth shoulders sprinkled with water droplets to the towel that began just at the swell of her breasts.

As her body shivered under his intense scrutiny, she saw him reach past her and pick up one of the hand towels that was hanging on a rack. "What's that for?" she asked, looking up at him.

"I don't want you to get a chill."

The sudden warmth in her cheeks had nothing to do with the heat of the bathwater. "You don't have to do that, Travis. I can manage."

"I know you can," he said, a half smile on his lips. "May I, Elizabeth?"

"Yes," she whispered.

Stepping behind her, he took a deep breath, his senses overcome by her scent, her nearness. With one hand, he gently lifted the damp curls at her nape; with the other, he blotted the moisture from her neck, her shoulders, her back, all the while savoring each lingering contact with her skin. The movement of his fingers momentarily stilled as he fought the urge to kiss the droplets from her skin.

She caught her breath at the touch of his hands against her skin, finding it hard to sit still, every nerve ending aware of the delicate touch that barely brushed her ears, smoothed over her neck and shoulders and traced the sensitive region of her spine.

She felt cold when his hand stilled, then drew away and the movement of the towel ceased.

"I should let you get dressed," Travis said, knowing that it had taken all his willpower to break the contact.

"I won't be a minute," she said, trying to ignore the sharp stab of disappointment she experienced as he edged past her.

He left the room, but her skin didn't know that. It was still tingling from his touch. She straightened the bathroom and got dressed, her mind reliving the last few minutes as she did so.

"I'm ready to go downstairs," she told Travis as she pulled open the bathroom door.

"When was the last time you slept through the night?" he queried.

"I don't know. I wasn't sleeping too well even before Rick and Kathy—before they left on vacation. I was too big, and I couldn't seem to get comfortable."

"Then how would it be if you moved back up here? The fire's going, and the heat's set. Ritchie will be fine. I'll sleep downstairs and keep him with me."

"Thank you." And then, acting on pure impulse, she pressed a kiss to his cheek. "That was for Ritchie," she blurted out, immediately retreating.

"And this is *from* Ritchie," he said, his hands framing her face. His pulse quickened as he inhaled the intoxicating scent that clung to her as lovingly as a second skin. His mouth found the sweetness of her lips.

"Good night, Elizabeth," he whispered, his voice deeper than usual. "Sleep well."

"You, too," she breathed, still somewhat dazed by his kiss.

No chance, he groaned inwardly. Back in the living room once more, he sat in the cushioned window seat, leaning his head against the icy glass. He needed a walk outside, frigid temperatures notwithstanding. Or a very cold shower.

"Coward," he taunted himself, the words bitten out. What he needed was to concentrate on his purpose—making sure that Elizabeth had a good night's sleep. But Travis had a hard time falling asleep himself. The baby was quiet. There was no sound coming from upstairs.

Somehow it didn't matter that Elizabeth was upstairs, half a house away, rather than downstairs, nearby. It didn't even matter that she was barely out of the hospital, or that he damned well had no business thinking about her.

His awareness of her was constant. In his mind's eye, he could still see her fresh-faced beauty. His hands remembered the silky feel of her damp skin. The tantalizingly brief kiss had left him aching, wanting more. And now, as he lay in her daybed, his senses registered her scent, her presence, even though she was nowhere near. He could almost imagine her lying next to him—beneath him—in the narrow space . . .

9

ELIZABETH WAS JUST waking up when Travis entered her bedroom the next morning.

"Hi. I must have overslept," she said huskily. "You must be exhausted."

"I'm fine," he assured her. "Ritchie's been washed, changed and fed, by the way. Don't move—I'll be back in a couple of minutes."

By the time she heard his footsteps on the stairs, Elizabeth had managed to put on her robe, wash her face and drag a comb through her hair. Just as she was getting back into bed again, Travis was coming back into the room carefully bearing a steaming cup of tea.

"I cheated," he admitted with a grin. "Used a tea bag."

"I'm not that much of a purist, Travis," she said softly, touched by his thoughtfulness. "Thank you."

"Can I borrow the keys to your van?"

"Sure. They're hanging up on a key rack in the kitchen. What do you need the van for?"

"I'm going to get the crib."

"I'll come down and watch Ritchie while you're gone."

He looked at Elizabeth, alone in her wide bed, then shook his head. "Not necessary," he said as he left the room once more. Within moments, he was back—with the baby in his arms.

"What are you doing?" she whispered. "He's asleep."

"I know. Scoot over."

"Why?"

"Elizabeth," he chided, "relax and scoot over."

After heaving a protesting sigh she moved over, and he set the baby down next to her. Then he propped several of Elizabeth's extra pillows on either side of Ritchie so that he wouldn't fall off the bed. "Now you two can keep each other company." He paused for a moment, captivated by the picture of mother and child together. "I'm going to get the crib from the house. I'll be back soon."

Leaving the tea untouched, Elizabeth edged closer to Ritchie—just to be sure he'd be safe, she told herself. . . .

OVER THE NEXT FEW HOURS Travis managed to fit in some time in front of his computer. And then he went back to Elizabeth's house to see how things were going.

"Ritchie's in the bassinet in the finishing room," Elizabeth said by way of greeting. "And there's coffee made in the kitchen."

Elizabeth seemed a trifle subdued, Travis thought as he poured coffee into a mug. Perhaps her mood was all part of the postpregnancy blues, he reasoned. Taking the mug with him, he went back into the living room.

He saw Elizabeth sitting on a low windowsill, her warm breath patterning the glass as she peered out at winter-whitened trees. He sensed her growing restlessness. "Elizabeth, I know you're restricted from driving. Are you also restricted from going out?" he asked softly.

She turned at the sound of his voice, leaning against the cold glass. "No. Why do you ask?"

"I just figured you might have a pretty serious case of cabin fever by this time. I thought you might like to go over to Brad's to do some woodworking. If you do, just say the word. I'll be glad to stay with Ritchie."

She sighed. "I'd love to get back to the shop, but frankly, Travis, I'm still a little ragged around the edges. I don't think I'd have the patience to work at the lathe, or even do some of the finishing work. If you really want to know the truth, I don't think I could sit long enough to get anything done."

"You're still sore, aren't you?" he asked gently.

"You could say that," she agreed, a wry smile on her lips. "And if I go at something when I'm tired, I'm apt to make mistakes. I wouldn't mind getting out, though."

"You wanna brave the elements? Wanna put on your boots and play in the snow?"

She blinked as she tried to follow his hopscotching questions. "I'd love to. And I think we could manage it if Louisa's free to come on short notice."

Louisa was only too willing, as Elizabeth soon found out.

AROUND SEVEN-THIRTY the doorbell rang, announcing Louisa's arrival. Elizabeth had donned wool slacks and an Aran sweater. "Ritchie's just been fed and changed," she said to Louisa. "We'll be out walking for about an hour or so. We're not going too far."

"Don't worry. We'll be fine," Louisa replied as she lugged in a book-filled canvas tote bag. "Enjoy!"

"What's our destination?" Travis asked after he helped Elizabeth on with her lavender down coat, then put on his own parka and gloves.

She tugged her knitted beret over her ears and pulled on leather-trimmed ski mittens. "Anywhere. Nowhere." She drew a deep breath, reveling in the crisp, clean air as she opened the front door. "I don't care where we go. As long as it's outside."

"Come on, then."

Travis was standing in the doorway, his hand extended to her. She put her mittened hand in his, and together they began a leisurely stroll, each word they spoke an icy puff that was visible in the breathlessly cold, crisp air.

As they walked, she ran her free hand along the top of a stand of snowy boxwoods. Feeling more lighthearted than she had in a long time, she flicked the snow, disturbing nature's pristine handiwork. And then, goaded by an irresistible impulse, she gathered some of the soft snow between the palms of both mittens, squeezed tightly and threw the snowball at Travis.

"You just wait," he growled, wiping the icy wetness from his already chilled face.

"No fair," she shrieked as she tried to elude the snowball he was shaping. "I can see from your snowball-making technique that you have experience in the art."

"Hey, we've all got to start somewhere, sweetheart." He cocked his arm playfully, a mock scowl on his face.

Travis feinted left; Elizabeth dodged to the right and felt her booted heels slide out from under her.

The snowball dropped unnoticed as Travis lunged, intent on reaching Elizabeth before she could fall. He just managed to catch her in his arms, their combined momentum putting them on a collision course with a tree.

The impact was softened as she was thrown against Travis's body. His eyes were locked onto hers; he was breathing heavily.

"Are you—all right?" he gasped.

She didn't answer, mesmerized by the reflection of moonlight in his eyes, and the flakes of snow dusting his hair with silver.

"Elizabeth?"

She could feel the pressure of his hands through her jacket, drawing her even closer to him, causing her to defy gravity as he pulled her along the length of his body. Her senses spun as he pivoted, gently turning her until her back was against the tree.

His hands were on either side of her, pressed against the sides of her face. All of a sudden, she was oblivious to the cold, deaf to the wind whistling through the bare-branched trees. The only reality was her body clasped tightly against Travis.

The first touch of his mouth on her own was as delicate as a snowflake. The kiss was endlessly changing—there was hesitancy, then tentativeness, then tenderness. He tasted of snow, of winter, but his mouth was firm and warm, bonding with hers.

Without releasing her mouth, he opened his parka, took her mittened hands, and slid them close to his body.

She didn't feel the cold. Instead, her face was warmed from his kisses. She shivered as she felt the warmth and weight of him against her, felt the heat emanating from his body—and the heat her own body generated in response. She stiffened, her response coming in uncontrollable shudders.

The unbearable sweetness shocked them—shook them both.

It might have gone on forever, but when he kissed her eyelids, he tasted snow—and felt her shiver. He saw from her accelerated breathing that she was flagging. "God, what am I thinking of? You're cold. Come on, Elizabeth," he urged, gently clasping her arm. "We'd better end this walk across Antarctica."

She wasn't cold; she was dazed by kisses of such overwhelming intensity that she feared even remembering them might alter the course of her life forever. Senses spinning, she could barely comprehend what had just happened between them—and now, something ending before it had begun. She only knew that she had come perilously close to intimacy.

She fought for control, waging an inner battle she thought she'd never have to face again: head versus heart. Her track record was dismal, her instincts lousy. Then she remembered the feel of him. Travis. The smell. The taste—all made up the man she couldn't forget.

He pulled gently at her mitten-covered hands.

She tugged her hands free and started on ahead.

"Elizabeth. Wait. You could fall."

She felt her face grow warm at the still-bright memory of what had just happened when she'd nearly fallen—and he'd caught her in his arms. "I'm cold," she lied.

He caught up, sliding his arm around her protectively. "We'll pretend the kiss didn't happen, if it'll make you feel better," he said in a low voice.

Even while slowly nodding in agreement, she was chagrined to find that she could identify only one response to his words: regret.

Why, she asked herself as she trudged silently alongside him. She shook her head as the unanswered questions whirled through her mind. Why this maelstrom of feelings? Why now? Why to her? And why this man?

"Are you okay?"

"Yes," she said, smothering a sigh. "Thank you for the outing."

"Thank *you*. I don't remember the last time I played in the snow." He certainly couldn't remember the last time icy cold had been so mesmerizing.

The rest of the walk back to the carriage house was silent, except for the crunch of bootsteps on snowy walkways. When they arrived home, they were greeted by Louisa.

"How was the grand expedition?" she quipped.

"Cold," said Elizabeth.

"Too short," Travis muttered.

Louisa arched an eyebrow at their out-of-sync responses as she began gathering up her things. "Right," she drawled, shaking her head in amusement. "Call me to baby-sit anytime, Elizabeth. See you soon."

After walking Louisa to her car, Travis came back into the house and offered to fix hot chocolate.

"No, thanks," Elizabeth replied, unable to see her way out of a fog of awkwardness. "I've got—things to do." Surely there was something she could find to occupy her time, she told herself in desperation. Trying to ignore Travis's presence in the background, she put a load of clothes into the washer and then dried the dishes that had been left in the rack. Finding nothing more to take care of in the kitchen, she roamed the living room, suppressing a sigh of relief when she found a ragged stack of newspapers and magazines that needed straightening out.

Travis watched her fumble around, knowing full well that she was whirling like a dervish doing minuscule tasks simply because she was trying to avoid him. Finally he called a halt. "You're going to wear yourself out running back and forth." What he really wanted to say was "running away."

"I'm not—"

"Yes, you are," he said quietly. He tugged at her hand as he led her to the sofa. "Sit. Please."

She did as he asked, making sure that she sat at least one cushion away from him, her hands clasped in her lap.

"It happened, Elizabeth."

She nodded.

"Was it so terrible?" Separated by the invisible barrier she'd erected between them, he waited anxiously for her answer. Maybe she'd hated it. She hadn't struggled, but then, he hadn't given her much of a chance to resist. Her emotions were out of whack; he'd had no right to exert pressure. But he hadn't been the only one doing the kissing. . . .

"No, Travis," she whispered.

"No what, Elizabeth?"

Deep breath. "No, it—the kiss—wasn't so terrible."

Damned with faint praise. "That's pretty lukewarm, Elizabeth. Too amateurish? Too sexy?" he prodded when she didn't answer. And still she said nothing. Behind her silence, he sensed wariness. "Too soon, Elizabeth?" he asked softly, his hand instinctively squeezing hers.

He almost missed the pressure on his own fingers and her soft-voiced reply, "Too used to a man who took what he wanted—and discarded what he didn't."

"I know one thing," he said, determined to break the somber mood that seemed to have gelled around them. "I've never kissed anybody I had a snowball fight with."

"Me, neither."

When she smiled at him, he felt his heart constrict in relief.

"I owe you a snowball, y'know."

"There's plenty makings for it outside, Travis."

"It's too cold outside. How about a forfeit?"

"What kind of forfeit?"

"This kind," he answered softly, bending his head and placing a light kiss on her nose.

AFTER ARRIVING BACK at Rick's town house the next morning, he listened to the messages on the answering machine. Frowning, he heard two calls from Leah Rabinowitz telling him that a system he'd only recently designed and implemented for a company in Tarreytown had crashed. And the client was a major one. The rest of the morning was spent on the phone with the client as he tried to resolve the situation by long distance. Finally, he was forced to admit that the telephone, modem, and fax machine simply weren't going to do the job. After arranging appointments with programmers at the site, he called Elizabeth.

Her heart echoed the night before. Her voice was breathless. She had to clear her throat. "Good morning," she managed finally. "I—er—you'll have to pardon the frog."

He smiled at the nervousness in her voice, and wished he had time to soothe it. "It's okay, Elizabeth. I don't mind frogs."

"I was thinking—maybe later today—"

"I'm sorry Elizabeth. I don't know how to tell you this, but I'm temporarily a nomad again, at least for a few days. Later today I'm going to be on my way to Tarreytown," he said, briefly sketching out the situation. "I tried to de-bug this company's mainframe problems from here, but I just couldn't. I've got to go to the site. I don't want to go, believe me." Remembering the way it had felt to hold her in his arms the night before, to feel her response, the last thing he wanted was to leave. "Will you call an agency this time? I'm not sure *I* can manage if I'm worried about you getting stressed, over-tired, overdoing—"

"I won't get stressed. And I'll work on not getting over-tired. I won't make any promises about it, though."

"What about cabin fever?"

"Travis, don't worry," Elizabeth cut in, laughing in spite of her earlier nervousness. "Jenny and Louisa will be glad to help out if I have a problem. And I'll be cleared to drive in another two days, so I'm not exactly stranded."

"I'll be back in time to take you and Ritchie to the pediatrician for his three-week checkup, don't worry."

Travis's absence scared her, not so much because she was alone. She would manage to cope, now that she was feeling stronger. And she could always call Jenny, after all. But she missed Travis popping in and out at odd times, and seeing how he tempered his masculine strength in caring for the child.

Although Travis called at least once a day, Elizabeth found that a voice over the telephone was a poor substitute for a flesh-and-blood man. But what really worried her was how much she missed Travis himself; she was afraid to become dependent on any man—and especially on one who was programmed to eternal wanderlust.

And what would it be like when he had to leave Ritchie at the last minute? Elizabeth asked herself with a shiver as she recalled her adoption agreement with him. Travis himself had told her that as the bachelor partner in his firm, his travel load had increased as his partners' families had grown. Would having Ritchie with him be enough of an anchor to force Travis to change his life-style and cut back on his travel?

She couldn't possibly let Ritchie go to a traveling single parent whose answer to the complications of child care was to hire a housekeeper. There was no way he could hire the kind of care that *her* son needed and deserved. When he got back they were going to have a talk, she decided....

TRAVIS'S ANXIETIES about leaving Elizabeth alone were considerably eased by the knowledge that Jenny was only a phone call away, and that Louisa could stay overnight, if necessary. Yet even as he was turning the car north and heading for New York, he reasoned that perhaps it was just as well that he was leaving Maryland temporarily. It would give Elizabeth and himself some badly needed time and space.

But leaving Maryland didn't mean that Elizabeth was out of his thoughts. Throughout his stay in Tarreytown, he was unwillingly reminded of her at every turn. When he used a towel in the bathroom, he remembered her scented dampness, the sweet curve of her neck, the water droplets he had longed to taste on her skin—one by one.... And when he walked outside, the snow under his feet recalled another walk. With Elizabeth. And kisses hot enough to melt ice.

Rather than being a source of relief, his nightly phone calls to Baltimore from his hotel near the Tappan Zee Bridge were catalysts that impelled him to pack four days of work into three sixteen-hour days. Finally, though, both he and the on-site programmers agreed that the problems seemed to have been solved, and the system was working as designed.

On the way back to Baltimore, he detoured briefly through Stamford to pick up his mail. As he walked through the door of his very modern condo, he was barely able to tolerate the sterile environment, the empty shell that he'd originally bought as an investment. He didn't want to live in an investment anymore, he realized as he shut the door behind him. He decided to contact a major realty company and list the condo for sale. And then he could get back into the car and head south again. Home to Baltimore....

10

TRAVIS'S HEART LIFTED as Elizabeth greeted him with a smile of unselfconscious delight—and a rather shy hug that he returned with eagerness.

"How's our boy?" he asked, sending a tender glance in the direction of the child who was sleeping in the bassinet.

"Fine. How was New York?" she asked, recalling her determination to talk to him about the amount of traveling he did.

"I packed four days into three to get back as soon as I could. And when I checked in at the office, I found out that the new guy's on board. He's going to pick up on some of the traveling. I'm getting kind of tired of this hotel-motel merry-go-round." He blinked at the brilliance of the smile Elizabeth sent in his direction. "What did I say?"

She shook her head, glad that at least one of her worries had been partially laid to rest: he was planning to reduce his time on the road. "I'm just—happy to see you. Ritchie and I both missed you."

"Well, speaking of you and Ritchie, I bought you a gift as I was detouring through White Plains."

"What is this?" she asked, once she had opened the package containing an odd-looking contraption made of denim, zipper and straps.

"It's called a Snugli. One size fits all, the salesperson told me. Even me."

"And?"

"And it's for carrying around a baby."

"I haven't had any trouble carrying him around."

"Ah, but you haven't been far afield lately, have you?"

"Um, no."

"It's a nice day out there. The thermometer's nudging forty degrees Fahrenheit. Let's all go for a walk. What do you say, Elizabeth?"

While Travis donned the Snugli, Elizabeth bundled Ritchie up warmly. And once he was securely nestled against Travis's chest, the three of them set out for a quiet stroll through the neighborhood. Like parents, Travis realized with a sensation akin to wonder....

AFTER NEW YORK, things settled into more of a routine. Several days after Travis's return, he and Elizabeth took Ritchie to the pediatrician, whose office was in the Village of Cross Keys. To their delight, Ritchie was pronounced entirely up to snuff, his weight right on target for a three-week-old baby and his yowls at being poked and prodded declared perfectly normal. Afterward, they went to lunch in the Village, and had a leisurely stroll amid the charming array of shops.

"Since your driving restrictions were lifted last week, and since I'm back now, I'm renewing my offer to stay with Ritchie while you go back to woodworking. Interested?" Travis asked.

"You don't mind?" she asked, hesitant but hopeful. "I'd only stay at Brad's shop on mornings."

Even if he had minded, he wouldn't have told her: the radiant look on her face would have kept him silent. "Why don't you take off this afternoon? And stay as long as you like. My computer's set up at the town house and my calls from clients are being routed down to Baltimore. So I could take Ritchie back to the house with me. He can help me work on a project."

"If there's any problem—"

"Just leave me Brad's number and the pediatrician's, Elizabeth. I'm sure we'll be fine."

TRAVIS BROUGHT RITCHIE back to the town house, setting up the downstairs powder room as he and Elizabeth had done in her house, so that he could change the baby. Who'd have believed it? he asked himself—Travis Logan surrounded by domesticity and diapers!

Although there was no one else there to help him take care of the infant, Travis managed to get quite a lot of work done. In addition to contacting clients and checking in with one of the techs in the Stamford office, he made one local call he could no longer avoid—to a real estate agent, listing the town house for sale.

When the phone rang, he thought it must be the real estate agent calling back.

"Hello, Travis."

Elizabeth. "How's the woodworking coming?"

"I'm finishing up a project that I'd started several weeks ago. Um, how are things with you and Ritchie?" she wanted to know. "It's not that I don't trust you—"

Travis leaned back in his chair, his stockinged feet propped on the edge of a desk drawer. "Everything's fine here. Ritchie's in the baby carrier on the floor right near the desk. He's been asleep a lot of the time. He doesn't say much. And of course, he opens his eyes every once in a while, looking at me as if he's actually—er—looking at me."

"I think that doesn't happen for a few weeks yet, Travis."

"Well, maybe our boy's precocious," Travis suggested, rocking Ritchie and the car seat gently with his foot.

At the end of the day, Travis was glad to see Elizabeth return tired but happy. But after several days of watching her drive off to Brad's workshop, Travis's curiosity got the better of him. He wanted to know what the shop was like, and what Elizabeth was like when she was practicing her profession. Of course, he could always ask her. But on second thought, it seemed to him that the easiest way to find out what she was doing was to go to the shop himself.

Leaving the baby with Jenny, Travis opened the door to Brad's shop and peered inside. What he saw was an eye-opener—an array of machines that looked like lethal weapons mounted on heavy wooden or metal tables. Racks held tools and pieces of wood in all sizes, and what looked like completed pieces were displayed on open shelving.

In the midst of all the noisy chaos was Elizabeth. In her work clothes, intent on the project before her. She was wearing sweatpants, a turtleneck sweater, and a dark blue coverall that hugged her body. Her hair was pinned up, her eyes obscured by goggles. Her hands were busy doing something to a bowl that was mounted on a heavy piece of machinery.

He saw how focused she was, how carefully she controlled the object she was working with. As he watched, fascinated, he saw that there was a certain rhythm to the way she worked, a certain pattern developing as the wood took shape.

Later, when she came to a stopping point and turned off the machine, he walked over to her.

"What are you doing here?" she asked anxiously, tipping her safety goggles to the top of her head. "Did something happen to Ritchie?"

"Ritchie's fine," he assured her. "I just wanted to see you at work."

"How long have you been here, Travis?"

"Long enough to see that you really know what you're doing. What are you making?"

"I'm making a bowl out of a solid block of cherry. The machine I'm using is a lathe. Would you like a grand tour of the place?"

"Very much."

She walked him around the shop, pointing out the heavy machines, the smaller hand tools, and even the safety systems. Then, to show him the kind of work she did, she slipped the goggles back on.

It made him feel humble and privileged just to be able to watch a thick wooden disk take on a fluid, graceful shape under the tutelage of her hands. To Travis, the result was nothing short of miraculous: Elizabeth had created a beautifully patterned bowl from a rough block of wood. He saw the way her hands stroked the wood—and wished they were stroking him, instead.

AFTER HIS VISIT to the workshop, Travis had an even clearer understanding of the importance of woodworking in Elizabeth's life and vowed to modify his own routine in order to give her all the time she needed to practice her art. Over the next few weeks, he often conducted business in her living room using a laptop computer and a modem, at the same time spelling her so that she could go back to her woodworking whenever she wanted, or take the naps that she still found necessary. He was there to share meals and to help her care for Ritchie.

Touching gradually became more natural. Their hands collided as they changed a diaper or gave the baby a bath. They kissed the baby good-night. And eventually, it became quite the usual thing for Travis to kiss Elizabeth hello, and for her to kiss him goodbye when he left. Neither mentioned— nor was able to forget—the bond forged by the fiery kisses they'd shared in the snow.

But each time he had to leave Elizabeth's house, he felt an almost physical wrench. And when he reached Rick and Kathy's town house, he felt even worse. It became harder and harder for him to leave at night, and for her to watch him go.

WHEN THE REAL ESTATE AGENT called with the news that several potential buyers wanted to see the town house, it was nearly two months after Rick's and Kathy's deaths. So soon, Travis reflected dully. He hadn't even wanted to think about what would happen when the place was sold. Now that it was going to be shown, he knew that he couldn't put it off any longer. He would have to do something about the contents of the house.

Before very long, he was weighed down by the magnitude of the task he'd set for himself. It wasn't just a town house he was clearing out: it was the remnants of two lives.

SOMETHING WAS WRONG with Travis; Elizabeth was sure of it, but she couldn't very well come right out and ask him what was bothering him. She sensed he was in a down mood, but she didn't know why, and she didn't want to intrude on his privacy. When he'd left yesterday he'd been quiet. Too quiet.

Travis had said he'd be out the next day, but would be at her place in time for dinner. She glanced at the clock on the wall. Ritchie had long since been fed and put to sleep. It was seven-fifteen and dinner was ready. Past ready. Elizabeth was debating calling him when the phone rang; she wasn't surprised to hear Travis's voice.

"I—I'm running late, Elizabeth. I thought I'd be through. I missed dinner, didn't I?"

"I'd say that was a good bet," she said coolly.

"I'm sorry. I got kind of—hung up here. Do you think you could do without me for a couple of days?"

Was he tired of involvement? she wondered dully. "Of course I can do without you, but—what's wrong, Travis?"

"Nothing," he said, brushing her off. "I'll see you in a couple of days."

There was something odd about his voice. Something just wasn't right. Travis hadn't sounded particularly friendly; obviously he wanted to be left alone. "Travis—"

"I'll call you," he said in even tones.

She almost added, "Not if I can help it." All this time she'd been lulled into a false sense of security, laying herself open for hurt. Certainly the man had a right to be on his own, by himself, if that was what he wanted. "Fine, Travis. I'll manage. See you when I see you, I guess," she said flatly, determined to stem the tide of hurt she felt at being shut out.

He heard the thread of pain laced through her voice, and knew he couldn't let her go until he'd made amends. "I'm sorry, Elizabeth. I didn't mean to be short with you. The real estate agent called the other day, so I knew I couldn't put off clearing out the house any longer. I've been sorting through things here, and it's taking me longer than I thought it would."

"Do you want help?" she asked, all too aware of the wire-taut tension underlying his words.

"I can handle it myself," he told her without hesitation. The last thing he wanted was that she put herself out, or strain herself. "Just don't expect me for meals. And call me if you need anything."

She didn't hear from him all that day, or the next. Not wanting to intrude, she didn't call him. Instead, she took care of the baby, ate solitary meals, which she didn't enjoy, and tried to draft sketches for a tiered rosewood curio shelf she'd been thinking of for a long time. But finally, she yielded to temptation and called Travis.

"Everything's fine," he told her, determined to keep going, to maintain a facade of control no matter what it cost him. "How are things over at your place?"

Lonely. Quiet. So cold that even a crackling fire couldn't instill warmth into it. "Fine," she replied.

"I'm glad you called, Elizabeth. I needed to hear a human voice."

"A human voice," she echoed once the brief conversation had ended. "You need more than that!" Putting on her boots and down jacket, she packed up all the necessary paraphernalia and bundled Ritchie into his snowsuit. "Come on, honeybunny," she crooned as she buckled the child into the car seat, "let's go see Uncle Travis."

When she opened the town house door with the key she still had, the place looked as if a tornado had cut a swathe through it. The place was an absolute shambles. Furniture in disarray, books and clothes strewn about everywhere.

Setting Ritchie's car seat down on the kitchen table, she began a room-to-room search. She didn't have far to look: in the midst of the mess in the living room, she found Travis sprawled in an armchair, looking so despondent, dejected, and broken, that it caused her physical pain. His eyes behind the fogged lenses of his glasses were dull, his face gray. More than anything, she wished she could put her arms around him and take the pain away. . . .

He hadn't heard the sound of a car drive up, or the sound of a key in the lock, but the next thing he knew, Elizabeth had materialized in front of him. He swiped at the moisture that seeped from his eyes, nearly dislodging his glasses in the process. He barely noticed when she very gently removed his glasses and set them on the end of the littered coffee table.

"What happened?" she whispered, kneeling down beside him.

He leaned forward, shoulders and head bent, his fists knuckled into his eyes. "I thought I could deal with this, I really did—but I can't. I can barely tolerate being in this place," he muttered, his voice laced with self-disgust. "And my tolerance hasn't improved with time. I'm sorry, Elizabeth. I didn't mean to involve you in this, but I'm sure glad you're here."

Dear God, she groaned inwardly. She didn't really know what Travis's normal behavior was. He'd always seemed so much in command. Now she saw with brutal clarity that Travis wasn't under control at all.

She ached at seeing him stripped bare of the stringent self-restraint he wore like a suit of armor. Now he was divested of it; all that was left was the essence of the man—bone, muscle, sinew, emotion, feeling. *He hated being in the house.*

She cringed, remembering the day after she'd come from the hospital—when she'd booted him out of her own house and virtually condemned him to come back to this place that he hated. "Oh, Travis—"

"It was my fault, Elizabeth."

"What do you mean? What was your fault?" she demanded, her fingers clutching at his forearms.

"The accident that killed Rick and Kathy."

"That's ridiculous! You weren't driving."

"But when they mentioned they were going to go on vacation, I suggested New York. And most of the time they were in the city, I was still on the road."

"They *wanted* to go," she countered, appalled at his reasoning. "They were in New York for a week and a half before—before the accident happened."

He ignored that. "Rick was the only close member of my family, and I took him—our relationship—for granted. I thought there would always be time to talk, to do things together. So I put my career first. And there was no time. Time ran out.

"I was too busy to come down here to Maryland. I was too busy even to drive them around when they were on my home turf, when they came up to New York. If only *I'd* been driving—"

His unfinished thought chilled her to the bone. If he'd been driving, all of them would have been killed. Rick. Kathy. Travis . . .

Elizabeth really saw Travis's grief for the first time—grief that had relentlessly oppressed him for so long. She opened her arms, intending to offer him comfort. He went into her embrace blindly, sinking down to his knees before her, drawn to her generous warmth as iron to a magnet. She felt him shaking as she put her arms around him in an almost maternal embrace.

"Stop it. You've got to stop it. What happened wasn't your fault. It just *happened*." Because she was without any close family, she understood how devastating this kind of pain was. And now there was no one for him, she realized. No one but herself, she whispered in the stillness of her heart. Without asking his permission, Elizabeth took over. The man was an emotional wreck, perhaps on the verge of a breakdown. *He* had needs, too.

His head fell forward, her sensitive skin feeling the rasp of his beard as his face came to rest at the curve of her neck. She held him as she would have held Ritchie, cradling the back of Travis's head with her hand for support. Her fingers tunneled into the caramel thickness of his hair, unconsciously massaging his head. "It's all right," she crooned, the tears streaming down her own cheeks. "It's all right to cry."

For an untimed moment, they swayed together in the slow rhythms of an invisible dance. And then she felt him take a deep breath, then another and slowly lift his head. She let her hands fall away from him, not knowing what would come next.

The backs of his fingers gently blotted the tears from her skin. Then his palms cupped the back of her head as his mouth went in search of her own. He had kissed her before in a gesture of kindness, of friendship. And he had kissed her in the snow in a moment of blinding passion that could have melted the ice from the branches of trees. This time, the touch of his mouth on hers was an exercise in sensuality. His lips spoke without words as he coaxed her mouth into a soundless conversation. Come. Follow.

Without realizing how or when, her hands found their way to his shoulders, then once more to the back of his head, where she exerted a gentle pressure so that she could return his kisses.

Her soft words and gentle touches helped him grieve.

The kisses and caresses they exchanged awakened feelings in Elizabeth that had been suppressed for a long time.

Dazed, Travis felt he was losing himself in her, and he sensed Elizabeth was about to lose her control, too. Not wanting to let passion overcome reason, Travis gently pushed Elizabeth away.

"Travis, what's wrong?" she said, her breathing uneven.

"I promised myself I'd never take advantage of you," Travis said between shuddering gasps.

She felt embarrassed and rejected; she'd found herself drawn to a man—this man—after such a long time. For a moment it irritated her that Travis was such a paragon of control. But then, as he sat, head bowed, fingers embedded in his thighs—shaken with tremors that had nothing to do with grief—she knew that desire burned as sharply for him as for her.

"I'm sorry," he said in an effort to cover the awkwardness that ensued. "You've got enough to worry about. Clearing out the house is my problem."

"Travis, you've had no relaxation since you first got to Baltimore. You've been all tied up with concerns about Rick and Kathy. About Ritchie. About conducting your business long distance. And about me."

She leaned forward, covering one of his hands with her own. "Since when is it engraved in rock that Travis Logan has to be strong all the time? Why is it all right for you to be there for me, but it's not all right for me to do the same for you? Why can't you accept help? It's a two-way street, Travis. Other people need to be needed, too," she whispered urgently.

"I never thought of that."

"I can take care of clearing the house out for you, if you'll let me."

Stunned, he sat back on his haunches, blank astonishment written on his face. "You'd do that?"

"Do you trust me, Travis?"

"Of course I do!"

Her heart swelled at his unequivocal response. "Then trust me to handle this," she pleaded.

"Okay, Elizabeth," he said with a deep sigh. "It's all yours."

ELIZABETH'S FIRST STEP in "handling" things was to call Jenny at eight-thirty the next morning.

"Elizabeth, how are things?"

"Oh, moving right along. Ah, I need your help—yours and Brad's," she said baldly.

"All right. When do you need us for—and for what?"

"As soon as possible, for as much time as you can spare. I'm helping Travis clean out Rick and Kathy's place."

"Oh, Elizabeth. Isn't that Travis's responsibility, though?"

"It's something I want to do for him, Jenny. Something I *have* to do. I can't tell you why—"

You don't have to, Jenny answered silently. *I think I can guess*. But aloud she only said, "We'll be there. Just give me time to get baby-sitting organized for the kids."

The "project," as Elizabeth had come to think of the house-clearing task, would begin the next day, since the real estate agent intended to begin showing the house as soon as possible. The first thing to do would be to restore order from the chaos that had greeted her. Then she would break the house down into its component parts, drawing up a battle plan for the "troops."

Over the better part of the next several days Elizabeth spent time at the house supervising the boxing of clothes, dishes and portable items. Disposal of the furniture would wait until after the house was sold, so the place wouldn't look empty. And she made sure that books, papers and personal things were boxed and taken to her own house, so Travis could look at them later.

Many times, she would take an item, hold it up in front of Travis and ask, "Do you want this?" And he would respond with a nod, or a shake of his head. And sometimes, he would get a certain faraway look in his eyes, and she knew that the object she was holding had triggered memories. Often, that meant the telling of a nostalgic story, opening the door of his life to her a little wider....

It was a relief to give the place a final cleaning and dusting in time for the real estate agent to show it.

TO THANK ELIZABETH for her help, Travis invited her to dinner at a four-star hotel, the Calvert Court, which was in downtown Baltimore, across the street from the Inner Harbor.

By the time she'd finished her hair and makeup, the face in the mirror looked back at her with unfamiliar elegance. Elizabeth dressed up for the first time in a long time, selecting a black velvet dinner suit and an emerald silk blouse with sapphire accents. A strand of lapis beads and gold links accented the draped V neckline, and interlocking circles of beaten gold dangled from her ears. By the time she'd picked up her gold beaded evening bag, she was hard put to recognize herself.

She barely recognized Travis, either, freezing in place when she opened the door for him. She'd never seen him in anything but casual clothes before. The tan wool suit made his hair, for once tamed into well-brushed order, look bronze.

"Are you going to let me in?" he asked, cocking his head to one side, resisting the urge to run his finger around the edge of a suddenly too-tight collar. To his chagrin, Travis felt like a schoolboy on his first date.

"I'll let him in if you don't," Elizabeth heard Louisa say.

"Thank you, Louisa. I think I can manage," Elizabeth said dryly, holding the door open for Travis.

He helped her on with her cloak, which was a rich chocolate brown with black braid trim and closures.

"You have the number of the Calvert Court?" she asked Louisa.

"On the board in the kitchen," the young girl confirmed. "Along with the other numbers. Plus Aunt Jenny's home if I have a problem."

"Elizabeth, our reservation's for eight o'clock," Travis reminded gently.

"Sorry. See you later, Louisa."

The dinner, in the romantic setting of the dark elegance of the restaurant, was the first date Elizabeth had had in a long time. And it was the first in a long time that had meant so much to Travis. Her loveliness made his breath catch in his throat.

They had crab soup served in individual tureens, medallions of beef, and some wonderful concoction that included raspberries and cream. There was also a bottle of Elizabeth's favorite Italian red wine. But elegant though the meal was, Travis couldn't understand Elizabeth's fidgeting almost as soon as they'd walked into the hotel.

"Is something wrong?"

"Why do you ask, Travis?"

"Because I'm concerned. You're picking at your shrimp cocktail and you've barely touched your wine. Don't you feel well?"

"I feel fine. It's just—" She broke off on a sigh. "It's just— I'm nervous."

"Being out with me makes you nervous?" he asked. "I'd hoped that after all this time, we'd be a little easier with each other. We've been through such a lot—"

"Travis," she cut in, "I'm not nervous about being with *you*."

"I'm glad," he said simply. "Then what, honey?"

Her heart skipped a beat, as it did every time an endearment escaped him. "I'm nervous because it's the first time I've left Ritchie with Louisa when I wasn't around."

"We're only about ten miles away," he said in an effort to reassure her. From her strained expression, he could see that his words had had little impact.

"I'm going to call home," she said abruptly, pushing back her chair.

He placed his hand over hers. "Stay."

She tugged at her hand. "Travis, let go." To her amazement, she saw him raise his other hand. In less than a moment, the hostess had come over.

"Is something wrong?" the woman asked.

"No. But the lady would like a telephone, if that's convenient."

"Certainly, sir."

"I don't believe this," Elizabeth muttered. And she was truly amazed when a portable phone was brought to their table. Moments later, she was speaking to Louisa. "How are things? How's Ritchie?"

"He woke up. I fed him, then changed him. Then I started reading him *Hamlet*—we're studying that in English class. He went right to sleep. Don't worry, okay?"

"I won't. See you later, Louisa."

"Well?" Travis queried.

"He's fine," she said, lowering her eyes. "You think I'm overanxious, don't you?"

"No. Just—" He broke off, barely able to call back the words he'd almost said—that she was simply acting like a mother. Instead, he said, "I think it's perfectly normal for you to be concerned. Do you want the hostess to leave the telephone?"

She shook her head, her fingers lightly stroking the stem of her wineglass. "I think once was enough," she murmured, lifting the glass and taking a sip....

After dinner, Travis led Elizabeth to a glass elevator, which they rode to the fifteenth floor as the city slid by in a blur. A walk down a thickly carpeted corridor led to a lounge, which presented a spectacular view of the Inner Harbor and beyond. But more exciting than the view was the parquet dance floor, where, to the subtle strains of a trio, he once more experienced the joy of holding her in his arms. She floated on air as Travis kept her close to his tautly muscled frame.

Caught up in the heightened sensuality of the moment, Travis gave voice to his innermost thoughts. "I'd like nothing better than to make love to you." Then he held his breath, cursing his own stupidity for going too far, too fast, and almost certainly frightening her away.

Elizabeth stumbled as she heard the words he had breathed into her ear. "Do you have a key in your pocket?" she asked, trying to make light of the moment, yet shivering within the grip of emotions she was afraid to name.

Relieved that she hadn't withdrawn from him, he put his arms around her, pulling her inexorably toward him. "I don't have a key." But he did have a kiss.

She turned weak-kneed, burning up, learning firsthand what it was to suffer from an erratic heartbeat. She was lost in an unfamiliar dreamworld, in which the thrust of his desire was her sole anchor. But suddenly the dreamlike images were replaced by the past reality of her marriage.

She had almost lost herself in the moment—lost herself in him. Dazed, she pulled away from him.

Instinctively, he stopped her with trembling hands, letting her see how shaken he was himself. He snapped back to reality, looked down into turquoise eyes that seemed focused on some distant point. "Come back from wherever you've gone. You went away from me."

"I want to go home," she said, expecting an argument, which wasn't forthcoming.

Putting his arm around her, they walked out. He turned up the heat in the car then asked, "Can you tell me where I went wrong?" When she shook her head, he took a deep breath, keeping his eyes on the road.

She glanced at his profile, seeing his tension. "It wasn't you," she said. "I'm sorry."

He nodded curtly.

The atmosphere of strained silence continued until after they reached Elizabeth's place. When he took her to the door of her house, he was stiff, like a stranger. She invited him in; he declined. She didn't want him to leave, so she asked for help putting Ritchie to bed, instinctively feeling he wouldn't say no.

Travis leaned against the door frame. "You don't need me, Elizabeth. Louisa's been here all this time. I'm sure Ritchie's fine, isn't he, Louisa?"

"He's been great," Louisa said, glancing from Elizabeth to Travis and back to Elizabeth again. "I'll—er—see you soon. Good night."

"Travis, please come in. I need to talk to you."

With a stiff nod, he closed and locked the door, and shrugged out of his coat, laying it on the back of a chair. To his surprise, she came over to him, linking his hand with hers.

"Come sit down," she urged, leading him to the sofa. "It wasn't you," she repeated. "It was—I guess I had a kind of flashback. To my marriage."

"You were married?"

"For nearly three years. Oh, God. I'm sorry. I'm not used to this. It's hard for me."

"Do I remind you of him?"

"No! He was petty, a put-down artist. You're *not* like him."

"I'm glad. You looked pretty fierce. Well, thanks for telling me. I'll go now. I don't want to wear out my welcome."

"I thought everything was all right between us," she asked as she saw him getting to his feet.

"It is."

"Then why are you leaving?"

"I have to, Elizabeth."

"You have to?"

"I can't stay. If things were different—" He swallowed hard. "I want . . . I need—" He ran a hand through his hair. "I want you too much," he said softly, picking up her hand and pressing his lips to her knuckles.

When she felt his hand begin to withdraw from hers, she tightened her fingers around his and returned the gesture he had just made. She bent her head, laying her lips on the back of his hand.

"Elizabeth!"

"Don't go, Travis. I want you, too. So much." Too much to let him leave.

"Are you sure, Elizabeth?"

"Very sure." And then, instinctively she divined that the only way to convince him of that was to breach the barriers that she'd erected so long ago. His hair, so well-ordered at the start of the evening, was once more in endearing disarray, falling onto his forehead. With a tender smile, she gloried in the freedom to brush it back, delighted when his head followed the movement of her hand. She embraced him, drew him closer to her, slowly but deliberately seeking his lips with her own.

He returned her kiss, touched that even though she was still hesitant, she was reaching out to him, seeking his warmth. Without knowing why, he realized that this was important to him, somehow. His muscles tensed at the tightening in his groin. The last thing he needed to do was frighten her with the force of his desire. . . .

His hands eased the velvet jacket from her, then gently clasped her silk-clad shoulders. His mouth pressed tender kisses above and below the delicate strand of beads she wore. Her neck fell back in response to each touch of his mouth on her scented flesh. And her fingers wove through his hair, pressing his lips even closer.

He could feel her breath catch and her heartbeat accelerate beneath his hand as he traced the draped V neckline that emphasized her full breasts. The blouse had no buttons, he realized as he lay her gently against the sofa cushions. The only thing holding the jewel-toned silk together was a tie at the side of her waist. A tie with only a simple bow that he unraveled with barely a tug. The sides of the blouse fell open in silken abandon, exposing her black-lace-covered breasts to his gaze.

"So lovely," he murmured, his mouth descending to her nipple as his hand parted the slit of the velvet skirt and palmed her knee.

"T-Travis!" she gasped.

With difficulty, he dragged himself back from very close to the brink. "Still . . . too soon?" he managed between shuddering breaths, willing to pull back for her sake. "I'll stop whenever you want."

"No, don't stop. It's just . . . it's been a long time."

"Is this safe for you, Elizabeth? Did the doctor say it was all right?"

"It's all right. I'm just—not very good at it."

"Feel my chest, Elizabeth," he said, placing her hand against his chest. "If you were any better, I'd be needing CPR."

He eased away from her, then lifted her from the sofa.

"Let's go upstairs."

She linked her arms around his neck, allowing her head to drop to his shoulder as he carried her up the stairs and into her room.

There was something earthy, sensual, seductive about the way Elizabeth looked as he lay her on the bed. The black bra contrasted sharply with her creamy skin. And the brilliant-hued blouse hung half on and half off her shoulders like the wings of a butterfly, held in place only by the deep, four-button cuffs.

He lifted her unresisting left hand to his mouth, brushing his lips against the back of it, tasting her wrist, then releasing the buttons on the cuff of her blouse, one by one. After doing the same to her other cuff, he slid the blouse from her shoulders and let it fall in a silken pool to the floor. It took him only moments longer to free her from the velvet skirt and black panty hose.

As he paused, her eyes held his, their turquoise depths a mixture of sensuality, innocence and, he hoped, anticipation. His gaze descended to her breasts, which strained against the taut black lace with every uneven breath she took. While his mouth and tongue blazed a hot, damp trail on the shadowy cleft between her breasts, his fingers released the front closure of her bra.

With delicate precision, his tongue traced the lacy patterns the bra had impressed on her pale flesh. While his mouth honed in on one dusky nipple, one of his hands stroked her bare midriff. He felt her shudder as his hand migrated lower, to her black panties.

Rather than pressing, he made calm, circling motions against the black silk until he felt her tension ease, and her breathing accelerate. "That's it," he murmured, the heel of his hand creating gentle friction at the junction of her thighs. Her legs shifted, opening slightly, as if in invitation.

"Lift your hips for me, honey," he rasped thickly. And when the slight movement came, he eased the panties down, exposing a downy furring of red gold.

"So lovely," he breathed as his mouth rediscovered her breasts, circling each nipple, sucking lightly. "Strawberries and cream. That's what you look like, pale cream and rose. And here," he said, his palm exerting a gentle rhythm at her delta, "here you're pure gold." Her hips started to move against his hand as his finger gently sought the treasure hidden within. He stilled when he felt her stiffen and close her thighs against him. "Am I hurting you?"

"I guess I'm a little scared."

"Do you want me to stop?" he asked, holding his breath. "No."

He continued his pursuit, gently, steadily exploring her inner softness, fighting to control his own response as he fought to give her pleasure. And when she arched against him suddenly and he felt her sensual wetness, he knew he'd succeeded.

She felt boneless. Damp. Everything tingled. Even her skin was sensitized, as if sandpaper had been rubbed across the surface. And yet, she was not complete. Coming slowly back to her senses, she became aware of Travis, lying over her, propped on his elbows, his legs on either side of hers. His jaw was clenched, his chest heaved against her breasts, and the pulsating hardness she felt against the junction of her thighs seemed almost to have a life of its own. As if of its own volition, her palm came up to stroke the damp roughness of his cheek. "Travis, aren't you—"

"Elizabeth. Wait." He pulled back. "I have to know something. Are you protected?"

"I'm on the Pill. Doctor's orders."

He gave her one last glance, then rolled away from her to remove his own clothes, not caring where they landed.

She blushed as more and more of his skin was revealed. Travis was lightly muscled, with a narrow waist and lean hips. And his shaft was hard and erect.

He saw where she was looking and almost groaned aloud as he got into the bed next to her. He lay on his side, turning so that she lay facing him, front to front. "I'm not going to hurt you, Elizabeth. Believe that, if you believe nothing else. If it hurts, or you just want to stop at any time, you tell me."

"That's not fair to you."

"Hey, not to worry. I can handle it."

Both laughed at his choice of words, the touch of humor defusing the tension. He slid his arms around her, drawing her to him, her soft breasts cushioned against the hardness of his chest.

She felt his finger probe her narrow channel, arousing her until the pressure built up from the inside out. "Travis," she begged. "*Please.*"

She lay on her back, and he held himself above her for a moment, his hot, pulsating shaft in readiness before entering her very slowly.

"Hurting?" he gasped, looking down into her teary eyes.

"Not—much," she murmured, as she felt the pain ebb.

"Liar," he whispered softly, bracing his arms as he prepared to withdraw.

She wound her arms around him. "No."

It required infinite patience on his part—and trust on hers—but then he was inside her.

"I could stay here . . . forever," he gasped as his mouth launched a sensual assault on her shoulder. He remained hard within her, his control so rigid that his muscles nearly locked. Never had he exerted himself so much for his partner's satisfaction. And then, at the last possible moment, his mouth found hers, absorbing her sensual cries before everything was lost in a suspension of time and space. . . .

Elizabeth woke to find Travis's tousled head on her breast, and his hand, wielding a damp washcloth, very gently soothing the unbearably sensitive area between her legs.

"How do you feel?" he asked softly, brushing the damp hair away from her face.

"I don't know if I feel anything except about as limp as that washcloth," she said, smothering a yawn.

"You *feel* wonderful," he said, drawing her close to him. "Elizabeth—" When there was no response, he knew she was asleep.

He'd wanted to tell her something. It would keep, he told himself as he lay his arm across her waist and tucked her body against his.

WHEN SHE AWOKE sometime later, he was still asleep. Except for the time he'd fallen asleep on the downstairs sofa, she'd never really seen him in repose.

Who was this man, this Travis Logan? And why did he affect her as no other man ever had? When he'd made love to her, she'd felt as if she were coming apart inside. Years of hard-won control had surrendered to pure need. And he'd been there with her all the way. To comfort her, to delve into inner passions she'd never explored, to make love to her with such patience and generosity that even to think about it caused her bittersweet pain. Even to stop—to withdraw—if his pleasure brought her pain.

But he hadn't withdrawn. And she'd accepted his love-making. No, *accepted* was the wrong word—and unfair to Travis. She'd *gloried* in it, and in the way it made her feel so much a woman. But deep down, she feared that the bond that had been forged could never be broken. For in making love to her, he had penetrated not only the tender flesh of her body, but the sensitive, inner core of her heart.

She felt her eyes drifting shut once again. For now, his arms were around her. Strong. Reassuring. She gave herself up to the feeling. To sleep. To him. On the edge of tears, she let herself trust. Believe. Dream . . .

SHE WAS STARING at him.

"Have I grown two heads?"

"Uh-uh. I was just wondering about . . . I don't know if you have anybody in your life."

"Huh?"

"A woman."

He stared at her. "Yes."

She turned white, edging away from him.

He followed, putting his arms around her.

She struggled against him.

"Hey, honey, ease up. There *is* a woman in my life," he said, his words punctuated by a kiss that coaxed her tongue into a dialogue with his. "You're the woman—the *only* woman—in my life." A last kiss, hard, hot, and deep, served as an exclamation point.

Her hand delved into the crisply curling hair that furred his chest. "I thought . . . you travel so much, I thought maybe you had a girl in every port."

For a moment, there was dead silence. Then he laughed so hard that the bed shook. "I don't know whether to be flattered or insulted."

Her eyes swept him. "Be flattered."

"Oh, honey, I'm no lady-killer. I'm just a science nerd out of the Massachusetts Institute of Technology. There was someone once. I tried—we both did, I guess. It didn't work out. Since then, I've dated, but I've never really had time for a long-term relationship. Maybe it's because I move around too much. Or maybe I just never found a woman I could commit to. Until now," he added softly, snuggling her into his arms again.

"What?"

Although he wasn't sure of her feelings, he was sure of his own; if he didn't say the words he felt, he'd explode. "I love you, Elizabeth."

Her hair brushed against his arm as she shook her head.

"What's wrong?"

She buried her head against his chest.

"Can you tell me what's wrong, honey?"

She swallowed hard, then drew back until she could see up into his face. "I'm not used to someone saying 'I love you.'"

"What then?" he asked softly.

"I'm used to the conditional," she said with more than a trace of bitterness.

"The conditional?"

"I'll love you *if* . . ."

"If?"

"If you get good enough grades, if you forget that stupid idea of woodworking, if you get into the right school—"

"If you make the right marriage," Travis cut in.

"Yes. That, too."

"Your parents?"

She nodded. "And my ex-husband."

"Ah, the man I'm so glad I don't resemble."

"No way," she declared. "Being a product of divorced parents, I desperately wanted my marriage to be everything my parents' marriage wasn't. Loving. Secure. Lasting. I wanted a family.

"I thought I would find all that with Dennis Chapman. I thought I loved him. Maybe he loved me, but not for myself. He wanted a good corporate wife. He constantly put down my woodworking—didn't consider it a proper activity for his wife. It wasn't 'feminine' enough. He wanted me to be an ornament. Dennis didn't want someone who was always lugging around big hunks of wood. You should have seen him pitch a fit when I hauled a burl of wood in the Mercedes he'd bought me.

"Given my mother and father's relationship with each other, I bent over backward to try to do everything right, giving in even when it went against the grain. I tried to conform to his image of the perfect wife, I really did, but no matter what I did, I couldn't please him. And I only succeeded in denying myself. Maybe my expectations were too high. And maybe I expected too much from him. I still don't know."

"Well, let me tell you something," Travis said softly, urging her closer and pulling the covers up over them. "My love *isn't* conditional, nor do I give it lightly."

"Travis, please—"

"Uh-uh, honey. My turn. I've never said the words to anyone before."

"But I—I can't say them back, not now."

"And I can't take back what I said. And I won't. I love you, Elizabeth. With no conditions or strings attached."

"You're just saying the words in the heat of passion."

"Remember, I'm just a science nerd. What do I know from the heat of passion?"

"A lot!" she said without hesitation, her cheeks flaming.

11

THE NEXT MORNING Travis went back to the town house, ostensibly to work. He didn't even turn on the computer. When he looked at the screen, all his mind was able to focus on was the night before and the woman he'd held in his arms. Even now he could smell her scent, remember the way her responses had ranged from shy innocence to a deep passion he'd never experienced before with anyone else. But though she had generously given herself to him, he didn't blind himself to a deep-seated wariness in her—a wariness that had been all too evident when he'd said, "I love you."

No wonder, he realized with chagrin. She herself had lost her belief in love, or maybe she'd never had it in the first place. And then, quite simply, he'd gotten it all backward.

First there was the baby, then "living together," then his declaration of love. In an amazingly short time, they'd managed to create a built-in family that wasn't really a family— Elizabeth, himself, and Ritchie. Then there was his virtually living in her pocket when she'd been used to being on her own. And last night, he'd shocked her by telling her of his love when she clearly wasn't ready to hear the words.

Maybe if they'd met in a conventional way, things might be different now, he reasoned. What was that old-fashioned word that was sometimes referred to in advice columns? he asked himself. Oh, yes, he nodded in satisfaction. *Courting*. Elizabeth needed to be courted. And he, Travis, was just the person to do it. He hoped.

OVER THE NEXT SEVERAL weeks, courting Elizabeth became Travis's most important project. Largely by force of will, he managed to cut back on the number of site visits, or schedule longer periods of time between them. Also, he was concentrating on solving most of his clients' problems by dialing into their systems and analyzing data long-distance. Which allowed him to make time for "Project Elizabeth."

Travis invited Elizabeth out on dates, often arriving on her doorstep flowers in hand. Sometimes they walked the charming byways of Annapolis, Ritchie tucked into her Snugli, or visited the National Aquarium in downtown Baltimore. A delightful spot turned out to be a small seafood restaurant just across the Bay Bridge in Kent County. The food was wonderful, but the main attraction of the place was the windows that faced the water on all sides.

And with Ritchie tucked into the Snugli, Travis took Elizabeth to one of her favorite places, Savage Mill, where they wandered through craft centers of all kinds. She was amazed when Travis cast a critical eye at the woodcrafts, picking them up, turning them this way and that, running his fingers over the finishes, and saying more often than not, "You made one just like it." Or even worse, "You could make it better."

"You're embarrassing me," she whispered, knowing that she was blushing.

"Why?" he asked with a shrug. "It's just the truth!"

After the third time he'd compared her work to the pieces at one of the craft centers, she dragged him away, trying unsuccessfully to look stern. Finally, they both gave up and laughed.

Later she was both surprised and delighted when he arranged for Ritchie to stay with Jenny Fairhall, then spirited Elizabeth away for the rest of the afternoon.

"Where are we going? Why did I have to get dressed up?" she asked, having acceded to his request that she dress as if they were going out to dinner.

"You'll see. Now just sit back and enjoy the ride."

She sat back—and enjoyed the ride—which led to the Calvert Court, where they'd dined several weeks earlier.

"Time for some 'itty-bitty sandwiches,'" Travis quipped as he escorted Elizabeth into the posh lobby and up the carpeted spiral staircase that led to the second floor. From there it was only a short walk down a glassed-in corridor to the Windham Room and Baltimore's answer to high tea.

"Oh, Travis," she breathed, touched and delighted that he'd picked up on the fact that she loved British high tea and all its old-fashioned trappings.

"I hope you like the place," he said as they were seated. "I called ahead of time and found out that the tea is brewed, not served in little bags, that the cream's from Devon and the scones are freshly baked every day. And I'm prepared to do my duty by cucumber sandwiches."

A soft-spoken waitress came and asked if they would like the full tea, or selections from the menu.

"Oh, full tea, please," Elizabeth answered immediately. "If that's all right with you, Travis."

"Fine with me," he agreed. "And we'll both have Earl Grey, if you have it."

"Certainly, sir."

The food was served with elegant precision. A bone china pot on a silver tray held the tea. Flanking the pot were a matching china sugar bowl and creamer, and a plate of lemon slices. The tray of finger sandwiches included smoked salmon on brown bread, wafer-thin ham on crustless rye, and of course, cucumber! An oval platter held a selection of tea breads and scones, accompanied by Devon cream, tiny pots of jam, and flavored butters. And a multitiered tray offered tempting selections of miniature cakes and pastries.

"Well," Travis asked, "is everything all right?"

"All right? This isn't *all right*. This is absolutely marvelous! I feel like I'm in another world," she said with a sigh, a dreamy look on her face.

"Are you there alone?"

She reached past the tray of tea breads and grasped his hand. "No, I'm not there alone."

This time Travis did have a key in his pocket. They went upstairs after tea, and feasted on each other.

Later she invited him to dinner at the carriage house. And after dinner, as they sat in front of the blazing fireplace, she asked him to stay.

"I haven't wanted to rush you."

"You're not rushing me, Travis. I want this. I want *you*," she told him as she put her arms around him and delivered a kiss that was so intense, it had his head spinning.

They didn't make it upstairs until Ritchie's cries woke them.

"I love you," he told her again, this time in her bedroom after Ritchie had been taken care of.

"Travis," she sighed.

"Don't worry about it," he said with a wry smile as he got into bed beside her and drew her close to him. "Just accept it."

Her response was so faint that he barely heard it. "I'll try."

The last time she'd said those words, it had gained him Ritchie—and entry into her life. Now, the words gave him renewed hope for the future, *their* future.

He'd been banking on that future when he'd called the Connecticut realtor several weeks earlier and put his condo up for sale. It was past time—long past time, he'd told himself. But it wasn't only the condo itself he'd wanted out of. It was the nomadic existence he'd pursued almost relentlessly from the time he'd left college. Somehow, the on-the-road life-style no longer seemed real to him.

Each time away from Elizabeth and the baby was more painful than before. It was harder, nearly impossible to achieve single-minded concentration. Since meeting Elizabeth, every time he'd been out of town on even a short site visit, he'd wanted nothing more than to be back home—in Baltimore. He shivered inwardly at the power of the innocuous four-letter word. *Home.* That was where Elizabeth was. Where his heart was. He wanted to be close to her, to be with her, to forge links, to make sure that shadows didn't darken her eyes; and he couldn't do that from several states away.

Wanting to surprise Elizabeth with a fait accompli—his relocation to Baltimore—Travis began apartment-hunting in the area during the times that she was at her workbench. He circled likely prospects in the real estate columns and ads. He went to see place after place, and all he got was an intimate knowledge of Baltimore and its suburban neighborhoods. He became increasingly frustrated as he tried to find a place that spelled "home."

Some apartments were too small, or too far away from where he wanted to be. Others were noisy "swinging singles" places; he ruled those out. He wasn't hunting for women. And some apartments didn't even allow children. "They'll make a great investment," he was told. He'd had enough of that in Connecticut!

Finally, out of desperation, he called the real estate agent who was working with him on the sale of the town house. "I need a place in Baltimore City or County. For now, I'm looking to rent, but eventually, I'll want to buy."

"I've got some very appealing condos—"

"No condos. Please. I'd rather own a house. And have a little ground," he added on impulse.

"I sympathize with your problem," the woman said. And then she added, "Since you're interested in a house, there's a really special place that just came on the market."

He replayed her words. *A really special place.* "Could I see it?"

"Of course," the woman replied. Within moments, an appointment had been set for eleven the following morning.

The house was on a tree-lined street just off of Falls Road.

"One and a half acres," Travis heard the real estate agent say. "There's a plot for a vegetable garden and flower beds for perennials. The former owners were amateur gardeners. The house has four bedrooms and two fireplaces. There's a garage, although it isn't attached."

As the agent showed him the house, Travis knew instinctively that although this place had some age on it, it was solid. He liked the stone facade, the large front porch made for sitting on, the roughly beautiful lot surrounded on three sides by trees.

He could imagine rooms of love and laughter, with Elizabeth settling in, imprinting the place with her own stamp, making the rambling house into a warm, snug home as she had done with the carriage house. And here, she wouldn't be renting, wouldn't be subject to the whims of a landlord. The place would be hers, his, and Ritchie's, he envisioned.

And there was plenty of room for sandboxes, swing sets, and a dog or two. He folded his arms across his chest, a smile of bittersweet reminiscence on his lips. There was even room for the one thing he and Rick had always wanted—their very own pony.

But it wasn't the house or the gardens that really fired up his imagination. It was the garage. Away from the house, away from neighbors. Big. As solid as the house itself. And roomy enough for at least three cars, or anything else of equivalent size.

The place definitely had possibilities—possibilities that began and ended with Travis's asking Elizabeth to share the place with him as his wife, and as Ritchie's mother. And the mother of other children, God willing. Maybe even a little girl with copper-fire hair like that of her mother . . .

Travis walked slowly back to the house, feeling almost as if he were taking a step into the future. The agent had probably never made an easier sale, Travis realized as he signed on the dotted line.

His first instinct was to call Elizabeth—no, better than that, lure her out to see the place on the pretext of taking the baby for a ride. And then, reluctantly heeding the voice of caution, he told himself that he would have to tread slowly and softly. He would have to convince Elizabeth that it was *her* home, too.

So Travis didn't tell Elizabeth about the house. He could imagine the look on her face when he asked her to share the place with him. The house was a symbol for the heart that pounded in his chest. He wanted her to love it as much as he did, wanted her to realize the seriousness of the commitment he was making. He didn't know how he could prove his sincerity to her—and then he decided to talk to Brad.

"I bought a house," Travis told the other man, visiting when Elizabeth was at home with Ritchie.

"You're moving to Baltimore for good, are you?"

"Yeah."

"What kind of place did you live in before?"

"A high-rise condo."

"Pretty drastic change," Brad said laconically.

"I'm not planning to live there alone."

Brad Fairhall's mouth lifted in a half smile. "Taking in boarders?"

Travis cleared his throat. "I bought the house for Elizabeth—and for Ritchie. I'm going to ask her to marry me," Travis blurted out.

The half smile on Brad's face widened. "What does Elizabeth think of the house?" he asked.

"She doesn't know that I bought a house, or that I was even looking for one."

Brad just stared at him. "She doesn't know?"

"That's right."

"How long were you planning to keep it a secret?" Brad asked wryly.

"Until it's finished. At least, until part of it's finished," Travis concluded lamely.

"What if she doesn't like it?"

"Well, Brad, you're going to help me make sure that she falls in love with the place."

"I'm no general contractor," Brad warned.

"No, but you're a woodworker," Travis replied cryptically.

"So's Elizabeth. She could do whatever you have in mind. I don't want to do anything she might not be happy with."

"Brad, you come out and see this house. I'll tell you what I want. And if you think I'm off base, I'll back off. Deal?"

That same afternoon, the two men drove out to the house, Travis letting Brad walk around the grounds and get a feel for the place. Then Travis showed Brad the garage, and told him what he wanted done with it.

"It's going to cost something fierce," Brad said, shaking his head.

"I'm well paid for what I do, Brad, and I don't have a lot to spend my money on. I really don't care what it costs."

"All right, Travis. I'll start drawing up a floor plan and ordering equipment. But I hope you know what you're doing."

AND IT WAS JUST AFTER he got a call from Brad saying that the house was nearly ready that Travis got another call, this time from his Connecticut real estate agent. She told him that she'd found a buyer who would pay Travis's price, but since the buyer wanted the deal consummated immediately, Travis's possessions would have to be cleaned out as soom as possible.

For the first time, he wasn't frustrated at having to leave Elizabeth. The sooner he took care of things in Connecticut, the sooner he'd be returning to Baltimore—and to Elizabeth and Ritchie—for good.

ELIZABETH MISSED TRAVIS, thinking about him all the time. The only time she was able to screen him out of her thoughts was when she was in the workshop, where losing concentration could mean losing a finger. When the doorbell rang, she rushed to the door, hoping that she would see him on the other side. Instead, she saw a woman she'd never seen before—a professional-looking woman complete with navy business suit and briefcase at her side. "May I help you?" Elizabeth asked.

"Are you Elizabeth Chapman?" the other woman asked.

"Yes, I am."

"I'm Ellen Wheaton. I'm a social worker with Baltimore City. I'm here in reference to the adoption of Richard Chapman."

Elizabeth sank onto the sofa, too numb initially to say anything. Finally, she took a deep breath. "Adoption," she echoed hoarsely.

The other woman opened up her leather briefcase and withdrew a file. "We're acting on a request for adoption proceedings to go forward. The name of the attorney handling this is Philip Snyder, and the prospective adoptive father is Travis Logan. Am I correct?"

"Yes," she said faintly. "Travis Logan." Then, "Why are you here now? I . . . Travis and I talked about the adoption issue so long ago, but we haven't really discussed it since."

"I would have been here sooner, but sometimes things move very slowly through the court system. Evidently, this case was sitting on somebody's desk for quite a while. I just got it a week or so ago. May I see the child?" the social worker asked.

Elizabeth had to force herself to respond, leading the woman upstairs, where Ritchie was asleep in his crib.

"He's beautiful, isn't he?" the social worker asked.

"*I* think so," Elizabeth agreed.

"You can change your mind, you know, Ms. Chapman. Nothing's been signed. And even if you had formally agreed to give Mr. Logan temporary custody, you, the birth mother, have a chance to change your mind within the first ninety days."

"That gives me an awful lot of power," Elizabeth stated flatly. "You mean I can just say no and that's it?"

"Right. Of course, Mr. Logan could go to court with a custody challenge."

Elizabeth barely had the will or the strength to get off the couch and lock the door when the social worker left. In its own way, the meeting with the woman had been almost as shattering as the trauma of Rick's and Kathy's deaths. Elizabeth went upstairs and picked Ritchie up, needing to cuddle him even though she knew she would be waking him from his nap.

In spite of the warmth of Ritchie's little body snuggled against her own, she felt frozen, as if hypothermia had set in. Her teeth were chattering at the combination of shock, betrayal and fear as she was forced to confront herself and her feelings.

Eyes closed, she felt the forces of nature pulling at her mind, heart and body as she remembered the trips she'd made to the nursery in the hospital. She remembered how she'd been drawn to Ritchie by what she now realized was a mystical union, a link that was as old as Time itself. Thinking about Rick and Kathy, she recognized that the bond between her and this child had been forged in fire. "Your parents had to go through so much to bring you into the world."

In retrospect, she realized that a mysterious kind of gravity had always pulled her toward Ritchie, even when she had first gone to the hospital nursery. No, even further back than that—when the doctor had placed her newborn on her stomach and she'd had to consciously restrain her hands from reaching out to him. But whatever that force had been, she hadn't acknowledged it, even to herself. Until now. That force was love. And motherhood.

"I love you, Ritchie." She had never said the words before, not even in her mind. Or maybe she'd been saying the words all along, but hadn't understood the language. . . .

Elizabeth felt tendrils of panic merge with her already frayed nerve endings. "I didn't know what it was to be a mother. I didn't know it would feel like this. How could I ever have thought of giving you up?"

She'd come to like being a mother; she'd come to love Ritchie. Without realizing it, she'd reordered her entire life around this baby who Travis was planning to take away from her. Now, she not only felt like Ritchie's mother. She *was* his mother.

For one desperate moment, she was sorely tempted to pick up the baby and run, to get as far away from Travis and his court documents as possible. But running never solved anything, she told herself as she sank back into the corner of the sofa. It certainly wouldn't be fair to Ritchie. And Rick and Kathy wouldn't have wanted that.

Travis must have known she would bond with the child, that it would be too late for her to give Ritchie up after all this time.

She remembered that Travis had told her that his life-style didn't lend itself to relationships. Maybe his whole relationship with her, including his repeated declarations of love, had been camouflage—a smoke screen designed to mask the fact that he'd always intended to take the child.

Travis had only intended to be nice to her until the adoption papers came through. And then she remembered what else the social worker had said: "You can always change your mind. You don't have to agree to this."

But if she didn't agree to it, wasn't she breaking the agreement she'd made with Travis all those weeks ago? she asked herself, agonized. *I'll do what you want, Travis. I'll—keep him for a while. Temporarily. Then you can take him.*

She'd said all that to him the day before he'd taken her and Ritchie home from the hospital. Now, her promise was tearing her apart. How could she fight him? How could she *not?*

And at the back of her mind, a traitorous voice was taunting, "If the baby disappears from your life, so does Travis."

WHEN TRAVIS GOT BACK from Connecticut, he stopped at the new house even before going to Elizabeth's place. The interior consisted only of painted walls and bare floors. And then, standing at a window, his eyes drifted to the garage. Brad had done his work well.

Bursting with enthusiasm, Travis went to Elizabeth's place, key in hand. When he used his key to open the door to her carriage house, he knew something wasn't right. The whole place was dark, but the chain hadn't been on the door. "Elizabeth?" No answer. He was worried. More than worried.

Scared, he took the stairs two at a time, finally locating her in the bedroom, where she was sitting in the rocking chair he'd brought over for her from the town house. Immediately, he looked in the crib, but Ritchie was ostensibly fine, on his back, gesturing at the mobile.

"Elizabeth?" When she didn't react to his presence, he sat down beside her and took her hands. They were ice-cold. He looked at her and felt as if he were facing a stranger. "What happened? Is it Ritchie? Tell me what's wrong?"

"I forgot my place," Elizabeth railed bitterly, pulling her hands away from his. "Caretaker to a child. I made the mistake of letting myself get involved." She got out of the chair, brushing past him as she left her bedroom and went downstairs. The last thing she wanted was to talk to him in the same room where they'd made love.

"I don't understand you," he said as he followed in her wake.

"I had a visit today," she told him as she curled up on the sofa.

"From Jenny?"

"No. From a social worker."

He stared at her, dumbfounded. And confused. "A social worker?"

"You look so innocent, Travis."

"Tell me about the visit from the social worker, Elizabeth."

"Nothing much to tell. She very kindly told me that the adoption proceedings were—proceeding."

"Adoption—"

"Right. You remember, the agreement we made in the hospital? Anyway, she wanted to make sure I understood my rights. That once the papers are signed, these papers," she rasped, pointing to the sheaf of documents on the coffee table, "I have ninety days to change my mind."

He picked up the documents she'd indicated. To his shock, he found he was looking through a set of documents with his name as the one seeking custody. "Elizabeth—"

"I know, you forgot all about this. Or maybe you were just waiting for the right time to tell me."

"I didn't forget," he sighed, raking a hand through his hair. "And there was no point in telling you anything."

"Bastard!" she grated.

"Elizabeth, the wheels for this were set in motion on the day before you left the hospital. You agreed to have temporary custody of Ritchie until you were satisfied I would be a good parent. And then you'd agree to the adoption. Do you remember that?"

"Yes, but I don't feel that way anymore. I mean, it's not that you wouldn't be a good father, but I can't give him up, Travis. I just *can't*."

"I don't expect you to."

"I don't understand you at all. You said you wanted to adopt Ritchie." The words slashed at her heart.

"I know. But things have changed, haven't they? You were the one who initially didn't want the baby, Elizabeth. If not for me, we wouldn't even be having this conversation, now would we? Ritchie would belong to somebody else by now. Two nameless, faceless people."

"Stop it!"

"You can't stop the truth, Elizabeth. Back then, I didn't know you, didn't know what kind of person you are. And you didn't know me, either. I think we were both trying to protect the child as best we could. You, by watching me like a hawk, to see if I was father material. And I had to protect myself and the child in case you changed your mind again.

"I don't have any hidden agenda, here. I simply couldn't take a risk with Ritchie's future, with his life. To me, his welfare is the most important thing. To both of us, I'd have thought. I couldn't afford to waste any time, Elizabeth. We've both seen what can happen—terrible things."

She knew he was referring to Rick and Kathy.

"I couldn't leave it to chance, Elizabeth. I didn't want my brother's child to be a casualty of fate. But I can't convince you of that, can I? What can I do to convince you that I'm not your enemy?"

"Don't fight me for custody," she told him. "You can't win. I'm Ritchie's mother."

"Oh, Elizabeth," he returned, "why can't you believe that the last thing I want is to fight you."

She only shook her head.

Clearly, Elizabeth had no trust in him if she truly believed he would have gone ahead with the adoption without telling her. Why couldn't she see that he wouldn't—couldn't—do that to her? "Dammit, Elizabeth! I *care* for you!"

"You care about Ritchie," she corrected, her voice carefully devoid of inflection.

"I guess there's no way I can prove that I care about both of you." He couldn't bring himself to use the word *love* and expose the raw feelings he fought to keep inside. "Some things you just have to take on trust." And it was obvious that she didn't trust him.

"You're just afraid I'm going to renege on my promise to give Ritchie to you."

"I wasn't even thinking of that. It isn't a matter of custody anymore, Elizabeth. I want Ritchie to be part of my life. To be my son. I've always wanted that. Haven't I proven myself capable of being a parent, yet? Hasn't the trial lasted long enough?" And when she said nothing, he pressed on. "Way back when we argued in the hospital after the baby was born, didn't you say you were adamant about Ritchie being part of a loving family—a family with two parents?"

"Yes."

"Okay. I have a solution that might defuse this argument about custody."

"How?" she cut in. "By making Ritchie a football, like in an 'amicable divorce'?" she demanded bitterly.

"No," he said with quiet emphasis. "This child should be with the two people who love him most in the world." Now he had her attention. He only hoped she would say yes when he finished. "Ritchie should be with you and me."

"Shared custody," she said dully.

"Of the child," he confirmed, "and each other."

"Each other? What are you talking about?" she asked faintly.

"I'm surprised we haven't talked about it before. It's the most natural solution to the problem. The best solution, Elizabeth. We can both care for him."

"That's your solution?" she asked incredulously. "How do you figure that?"

"We can be those loving parents you described—if you marry me, Elizabeth."

"What?" she squeaked.

The look on her face was priceless. If the subject hadn't been so serious, a part of his heart, he might have laughed. "Instead of making Ritchie a 'football,' we can make him part of a family. *Our* family. Yours and mine."

"He already is part of both our families."

"We can get married, Elizabeth."

She stared at him in disbelief, barely hearing the words as he tried to convince her of the benefits of his idea. "No."

"Don't say no. Just hear me out. If we married, Ritchie would have two parents, two people who obviously care about him, who always have his welfare in mind. We could be a real family, Elizabeth. And neither one of you would ever want for anything financially, or—"

She shrank from his cold-blooded proposal for what was essentially a marriage of convenience—a proposal that did nothing to increase her trust in him. He'd never been married, and clearly his only reason for marrying now was the baby. She never considered that it could be *her*. "I know you're well-off, Travis, much better able to provide for Ritchie than I am. But don't think you can buy me or Ritchie." She didn't have to ask him not to buy her love: he hadn't mentioned love at all.

"That isn't what I meant."

"I don't want any part of a long-distance marriage," she objected, thinking that would stop him.

"Please," he begged, devastated by her refusal, "give the idea a chance."

"I hate the idea of it. I gave marriage a chance once before. I would never dare risk it again. I barely survived the first time."

"You haven't survived, not really. Your heart's buried in a deep freeze," he stated bitterly as he swallowed the acid taste her rejection had caused. He had so very much wanted her to say yes. "You've got this beautiful house, Elizabeth," he said quietly, with a sweeping gesture.

"It isn't even mine. It's rented."

"I know that. But you've given it your own touch, with the way you've furnished it. It's easy on the eye, and its comfortable at the same time—"

"I don't know where you're going with this, Travis."

"The thing is," he continued, ignoring her interruption, "no matter how beautiful this place is, you don't really have a home here, anymore than I had one in Connecticut. What you've got is an empty nest."

"I don't understand you."

"I'm not surprised. You live in this place that had all the comforts of home, but when it came to filling it, you've weaseled out."

"That's enough!"

"Uh-uh. Not quite. You wanted a family. So you decided to make this arrangement with Rick and Kathy, to take the easy way out."

"Just what does that mean?"

"You would have the trappings of family without having to make any long-term commitment."

"What about carrying the child for nine months? You don't think my having their baby was a commitment?"

"Sure it was a commitment, but one you'd planned to walk away from. Ritchie was supposed to be part of Rick and Kathy's family. You avoided the risks of a real commitment—of having your own family—by having a baby for someone else. You only wanted a family on a part-time basis.

"Your bearing a child for Rick and Kathy and being part of *their* family was a substitute love. You'd allow yourself to love them and the family you helped them create, but only from the safe distance of an outsider. You weren't about to risk the commitment to a family of your own.

"I should have known," he muttered. "I should have known what to expect when you'd never say you loved me. Even when the passion between us threatened to set the sheets on fire, you never said the words. And like a fool, I kept hoping to hear those words from your lips."

"That has nothing to do with this."

"You're wrong, Elizabeth. It has *everything* to do with it. If you really believed that I loved you, you'd know I could never do anything like suing for custody. But you don't believe it, do you?"

"I wanted to. You'll never know how much I wanted to. What about you, Travis? If not for the baby, you wouldn't be here at all. We wouldn't have met. After all, you're a 'tech-nomad.'"

"A what?"

"I just coined a word. It means a computer genius who makes his living on the road. I think the description is pretty apt, don't you? After all, you never managed to find the time to visit Rick and Kathy. Maybe your feeling for the baby is just a passing fancy, too." When she saw his jaw lock and his fists clench, she knew she'd gone too far. "Travis—"

"You aren't the only one who wanted to be part of a family, Elizabeth, especially since Ritchie was born." And most especially since *she'd* come into his life. "I've wanted that as much as you did. And I've wanted a place to call home."

When he saw no reaction to what he'd just said, Travis realized that Elizabeth had retreated behind a wall of hurt that he had no idea how to breach. The fabric of their relationship was torn beyond repair. Everything he said seemed to have led them further into emotional quicksand.

Before his eyes, he'd watched her change into a stranger. And he was hurting her; and her pain made *him* hurt. There was no percentage in trying to fight for Elizabeth on this; there would be no winners, only losers. "Enough. I've said enough," he bit out. "I can't go through with this. I'm withdrawing my adoption petition. There won't be any joint custody request, either. I'll have the lawyer draw up the papers and send them to you."

Jamming his bunched fists into his pockets, his fingers clenched around the keys to the new house, the metal ridges biting into his palm. He froze in midstep, then walked away from her without saying anything about the house, which to him represented the ultimate commitment to permanence. She'd just said she didn't want anything from him. Why would she want a house? She'd already accused him of trying to buy her; she'd probably consider the house a bribe.

His shoulders hunched, head bowed, he climbed the stairs to spend some time with the last remaining member of his family.

12

HE WALKED INTO THE ROOM and leaned over Ritchie's crib. The baby was asleep. Disappointed, Travis had to resist the urge to pick him up. Instead, he leaned his forearms on the rail and pitched his voice at the level of a whisper.

"I love you, Ritchie," he told his brother's son. "I want you to have a good life, like your daddy would have wanted. It's what *I* want for you, too. And for your mommy. I wish I could stay and watch you grow up. But we can't always have what we want."

Reaching over the rail, Travis brushed his thumb gently across Ritchie's soft cheek, then straightened the blanket over him. "I'll always come back if you need me."

He wanted to stay longer; he knew Elizabeth wouldn't have stopped him. But staying longer would only have compounded the hurt he felt inside. And it was pure torture to be in such proximity to her; he could only hazard a guess at the emotions she held in check behind the shuttered look on her face. The social worker's visit, the bitter words that had been said in its aftermath, and the coldly formal exchange since then had created a rift that seemed to grow wider and deeper and more painful the longer he stayed. This time, he'd come up with a problem that couldn't be solved by computer emulation or enhancement.

What tore at him most was the realization that without the baby to tie them together, Elizabeth would cease being a part of his life. In losing the child, he would be losing not only the last of his family, but Elizabeth, as well.

Dreams die hard, he told himself as he left her room. Travis loved Ritchie with all his heart. He wanted to see him, have a role to play in his future. But he didn't want sole custody of the child. What he really wanted was sole custody of Elizabeth. Instead, they'd become bitter adversaries.

Travis came downstairs composed. Strained. Calm. Ice. "I'm leaving tomorrow," he told Elizabeth, who was on the sofa in the living room.

"Where are you going?"

"Why are you asking?"

"I should know, if something comes up with Ritchie."

"You can reach me through the office in Connecticut. You have the numbers?"

"Yes," she whispered.

"Call me if you need me."

"You're going on another road trip? You just got back."

"That isn't any of your concern any longer, is it?"

"I'm sure I'll—we'll manage," she said stiffly.

Numb, Elizabeth watched him pick up his parka and turn toward the door.

"If you need me . . ." he said, turning back to her at the last minute. *Please, ask me to stay,* he pleaded silently. When she said nothing, he opened the door and walked out.

Steeling himself to endure the inevitable pain, Travis drove past the new house on the way back from the lawyer's office. The house Travis had hoped would mean a new beginning for the three of them was now just one more place that wasn't home. His dream of a family life—the kind of life Rick and Kathy had planned—died hard, too. As did his dream of love, he acknowledged grimly as he drove back to the town house to pick up his things and head back to Connecticut.

He had no idea where he was going to stay; the condo was no longer his. He didn't much care; a motel was fine with him. Yet another impersonal place.

Before leaving the town house, he called the office.

Leah sounded harried. "I was just going to call you. There's a crisis at Henderco in Chicago. I've got stacks of messages, none of them good. The system crashed."

"Damn," he muttered, remembering what it had taken to get the system up and running in the first place.

"Jack or Kevin can be free to go by the end of the week."

"I'll go today," he said without hesitation.

"But you just got back," she protested.

Strange how her remark echoed what Elizabeth had said. "It's okay, Leah. I'll get the next flight to Chicago out of Baltimore-Washington International. I'll be in touch."

Within two hours, he was at the airport, waiting for his flight to be called. After boarding, Travis leaned back in his seat, his gaze ostensibly directed to the planes that were taking off from the nearby runway. But in reality, his thoughts were far away from the miracle of man and machine defying gravity.

His eyes unfocused, he was lost in thought, lost in remembering his words to Elizabeth, "If you need me . . ." Why couldn't she have needed him? he wondered bitterly. It would have given him an excuse to stay. No. What would have been gained? It would only have prolonged the agony of knowing that Elizabeth and the baby would be a unit, while he would be left on the outside looking in. He'd wanted so much to be let into the golden circle of family and to find, as his brother had found, a woman with whom to share it all.

Now he had finally accepted the bitter truth: it *wasn't* going to happen—not now, and certainly not with Elizabeth. It was better that he get on with his life. And she with hers. And Ritchie. Ritchie would be with his mother.

It should have been easy for him to leave. Leaving was second nature. He'd done it so many times before. Being rootless was the way he'd functioned for longer than he cared to remember. But it had never hurt before he'd met Elizabeth.

ELIZABETH WONDERED what would happen next, but was too drained to do anything but take care of the baby and worry the night away. The next afternoon, she received a letter from Philip Snyder, the lawyer, asking her to come and see him at his office at her earliest convenience. She called and made an appointment for nine o'clock the following morning, telling herself that all she wanted was to get it all over with and get on with her life.

After a markedly cool exchange of greetings, the lawyer glanced down at notations on a yellow legal pad. "I'm to inform you that Mr. Logan is abandoning all efforts aimed at seeking custody of the minor child, Richard Chapman. Mr. Logan will want to visit the child, of course, at mutually convenient times. He will provide you with advance notification. Is that satisfactory, Ms. Chapman?"

"Yes."

"And Mr. Logan will set up a trust fund for Richard Chapman, based on monies derived from the estate, as well as the proceeds from the sale of the Logan town house. All right so far?"

She smothered a sigh at the formality of the legal language the lawyer was using. "Yes."

"And Mr. Logan will set up an expense account for you to use as—"

"No! Absolutely not. I won't accept any money from Travis for my own maintenance. I'm not poor. I wouldn't have accepted money from Rick and Kathy for bearing their child, and I won't accept any money from Travis to care for and raise my own child."

"You don't have that option. According to Mr. Logan's instructions, you either agree to the support, or, and I'm quoting, 'We'll have a duel, with lawyers at twenty paces. Don't fight me on this, Elizabeth. You won't win.' End quote, Ms. Chapman. Well?"

She didn't have to access the funds he'd provided; they could simply sit in the account and accrue interest, for all she cared. "Next item on your agenda," she said, deciding not to argue the point.

"I'm instructed to inform you that Mr. Logan is providing you with monies for top-of-the-line health insurance, and I'd advise you not to turn it down. You don't qualify for group coverage, and comprehensive care is expensive."

"I haven't had that kind of coverage."

"You haven't had a child before. You can't know what's around the corner. This will be a comprehensive family policy for both of you."

"Is that all?"

"I have papers for you to sign," he said, sliding several documents across the table. "There's a document relinquishing custody, a paper acknowledging formation of the trust fund for the child, the expense account for you, and another outlining the insurance coverage."

Elizabeth signed all of the papers, then slid them back. "Thank you for your time, Mr. Snyder."

"You can't leave quite yet. There's one more item. A house."

"You mean the town house?"

"No, I mean the house Mr. Logan recently purchased."

She sank back into the chair. "He bought...a house? I don't know anything about it."

"You will," the man sitting across from her said wryly. "Your name's on the deed."

"That's impossible!"

"Almost anything's possible."

"I already have a house."

"But you don't own it, do you? You only rent it. And it can be sold at the whim of the person who holds the deed."

"Yes," she admitted grudgingly.

"And even if the house you live in was for sale, could you afford to buy it?"

"No."

"Look, Ms. Chapman, my client simply wants to make sure that Richard is in a good home, that he is adequately provided for."

"And my house isn't good enough?"

"You might find yourself in difficult straits if the entire piece of property went on sale."

"I don't want a house. I can't afford it."

"That's all taken care of." He picked up a key ring, then pressed the keys into her unresisting hand. "The address of the house is on the deed, which you have to sign."

Her hand clenched into a fist around the keys as she looked down at the paper, scanning it. "It's got only *my* name on the deed."

"That's what Mr. Logan wanted. He'd originally had both your name and his on the document. He had me take his name off."

She felt as if she were getting divorced—without having been married. Her visit with the lawyer had had all the elements—custody, monetary support. She was even getting the house.

MORE THAN A LITTLE disturbed by Travis's presumption at buying her a house, Elizabeth spent what remained of the morning with Ritchie; even he seemed to miss Travis. And later in the day she went to the workshop but she found herself unable to concentrate. The one place she had always been able to screen out the world was no longer a safe haven.

There was neither joy in what she was doing nor satisfaction in the end products she did manage to turn out. And she had just set aside a halfway decent effort on a wooden bowl, when she turned—and watched in horror as the bowl tottered at the edge of the worktable and fell off, shattering. Just like her heart.

She looked down at the wooden shards, which multiplied as they were refracted through tears of frustration.

Hearing the sound, Brad turned just in time to see what had happened. He shut off the machine he was working on, and taking off his goggles, he went over to Elizabeth and led her to a nearby stool. "You're wrecking my shop," he said calmly.

"S-sorry."

"Why are you crying? You've been dragging for the last few days."

Dragging, she groaned inwardly. Travis had barely left, and already she missed him. And it was only this morning that she'd learned about the house he'd put in her name. She searched frantically for an answer. "I'm just a little tired, that's all. Postpartum blues."

"You look as if you've lost your best friend," he said, eyes narrowed.

Elizabeth shrugged. "I'm doing fine."

"That's a matter of opinion. As a matter of fact, I'm wondering why you're still working here."

"Does this mean you ... don't want me here?" she asked incredulously.

"Of course not! I mean, why are you here if you have your own shop?"

"Brad, I think you're losing it, I really do. What's Jenny been feeding you? For the life of me, I can't figure out what you're talking about."

"Travis didn't show you?"

"I haven't seen Travis since he left. And in answer to the question you didn't ask yet, I don't even know if he's coming back."

"Not coming back? That's crazy! He's planning on settling in Baltimore. He bought this house for you and the kid and himself. I was almost as excited about the place as he was. Heck, I was sure he was going to ask you to marry him."

"He did." And at Brad's look of confusion, she added, "I said no."

"If I live to be a hundred, I will never, ever, understand women," Brad muttered, shaking his head. "Do you know about the house?" At her stiff nod, he asked her if she'd seen it.

"No. Travis's lawyer gave me the keys, but I haven't been there."

"Do you happen to have the keys with you?" When she nodded again, he said, "C'mon, I want you to see this place."

Elizabeth said very little on the drive to a large stone house in northwestern Baltimore County. With the baby securely tucked into the Snugli, she followed Brad through empty rooms. And then she noticed the heavy-duty computer surge suppressor in the corner, and several strips of orange grounded plugs of the kind Travis used for his equipment at the town house. He really *had* intended to live in this house, as both Brad and the lawyer had said.

After Brad showed her the house, he led her to the garage. Except that it wasn't a garage any longer, Elizabeth acknowledged, her mouth dropping open. Before her was a state-of-the-art workshop that was outfitted as well as or even better than Brad's. Arranged in a circular pattern to accommodate work flow were a massive wooden worktable, a table saw, and a jointer. Against one wall were several other machines including a lathe and a band saw. The opposite wall accommodated a massive workbench.

There was also a locked metal cabinet, storage space for a selection of basic and exotic woods he'd provided, racks for tools, and a door that led to a smaller room. As she explored, she found that he'd even provided her with a finishing room, so that after a piece had been sanded down, its hand-rubbed finish could be applied in a dust-free environment.

"I'm in shock," she said finally.

"This was all Travis's idea. I just supplied the know-how. What do you think of it?"

"What could I possibly think of it? It's fabulous. It's what I've always wanted."

She couldn't believe Travis had done all this for her. But for who else? He'd never even told her. She screened out the sound of Brad's voice, still overwhelmed by the magnitude of what Travis had done. She didn't know why Travis had done this; she couldn't ask him. And she didn't need to hear Brad telling her how happy Travis had been with the planning, how impatient he'd been for her to see the finished workshop.

Bemused, accompanied by Brad, she left the unoccupied house. Once back at Brad's house, she put the baby in Vince's crib and went in search of Jenny.

"Not going to work?"

"Why should I?" Elizabeth asked. "Like Brad says, I have my own workshop now."

"How was your visit to the house?" Jenny asked Elizabeth.

"You knew about all of this, didn't you?"

"Brad and I don't have secrets. What do you think of the house?"

"It's fabulous. What I've always wanted."

"I think you'd sound as enthusiastic if I'd told you that beavers have been dining on your woodpile."

"I'd better take Ritchie and go home."

"Ritchie's asleep. If he wasn't, you'd be hearing from him. He's fine. Which is more than I can say for *you*. How about some tea?"

"The universal panacea. Sure, why not?"

"Do you want to talk about it?" Jenny asked, breaking an uncomfortable silence.

Elizabeth shrugged, taking a sip of too-hot tea and burning her mouth in the process.

"Is not talking about it doing any good?" Jenny prodded.

"No, I guess not," Elizabeth said, sighing.

"I'm here to listen."

"And to tell me where I went off the track?" Elizabeth laughed wryly. "A social worker came to the house the day before yesterday. With adoption papers. Travis had a lawyer start adoption proceedings."

"Recently?"

"No," Elizabeth conceded. "When I was still in the hospital, after I'd agreed to let him have custody of Ritchie."

"Isn't that what you had in mind all this time anyway?"

Elizabeth recalled only too well her conversation with Jenny, when the other woman had told her to hold off on making a decision about giving up Ritchie. "You can say I told you so, if you want."

"Friends don't say that, Elizabeth. You had a change of heart."

"I don't know when it happened."

"Kids grow on you, like mold."

"That's a lovely simile, Jenny."

"It's true, honey. Sure, some mothers bond with their baby immediately after birth, but not everyone does. I bet it said something like that somewhere in that pile of baby books you and Kathy read."

"Jenny it's like I've been in some kind of time warp, and I woke up with somebody threatening to take away my baby. I didn't want my baby to be taken away. I can't—"

"And your claws came out."

"Long and sharp."

"At the social worker?"

"No," she said after a long pause. "At Travis. We'd become so close. I couldn't believe he would do this to me."

"Tell me what happened."

Taking a sip of the rapidly cooling tea, Elizabeth told Jenny what had happened two days earlier. "He asked me to marry him, Jenny, and I said no. I—I thought he just wanted to ensure custody of Ritchie. But when I offered joint custody, he said no."

"Elizabeth, he *did* want joint custody."

"What!" she gasped, staring at Jenny.

"Travis didn't want sole custody of Ritchie. He wanted joint custody of Ritchie *and* Ritchie's mother."

"But the social worker—"

"Elizabeth, I seriously doubt Travis knew that a social worker would end up on your doorstep. But even if he did, there still would have to be one involved."

"Why?"

"Because Travis will want to adopt Ritchie when he marries you."

"That's not likely to happen—not now. He left. And he's not coming back."

"He's come back all the other times," Jenny pointed out reasonably.

"Not this time. He didn't even tell me where he was going. He's always going . . ."

"Did you ask him to stay?"

"It's not my right."

"Maybe it's time you asserted some rights."

Elizabeth remembered the way he'd stood motionless at her door. "If you need me . . ." he'd said.

"Is it really the traveling that bothers you, or is that just an excuse, like the visit from the social worker, to push Travis away?"

"What do you mean?"

"What did Travis say about the social worker?"

"That he didn't know, that he didn't want to take Ritchie away. That the best thing would be joint custody. He said we could get married," she mumbled.

"Right. What are you afraid of, Elizabeth?"

"Of failing again, of not measuring up. I was terrible at marriage, Jenny. I never wanted to do it again. I'm scared of taking the risk. Travis said I didn't have the guts to commit to anyone. I want to, Jenny."

"I'm the wrong one to tell."

"What if he won't listen?"

"If you want him badly enough, you'll find a way to convince him to take that risk."

Risk. The word echoed in Elizabeth's head long after she'd collected Ritchie and taken him home.

She'd decided to risk loving Ritchie. No, she admitted; the decision had had nothing to do with her. She couldn't *not* love him. And she couldn't not love Travis, either. She'd been fighting it for so long. Because loving meant she'd have to let him into her life, to crack the shell of safety she'd built, to take the ultimate risk with someone who was a footloose fancy-free bachelor—but was he?

He'd put himself at her beck and call, hadn't been afraid to get his hands dirty when other men would have simply gone running, or whipped out a checkbook. He'd turned his life inside out, asking for nothing except love, commitment, trust—and been slapped in the face.

Was their relationship like the bowl that had shattered in Brad's workshop? What was so wonderful about living in a shell?

SHE RETURNED to the unoccupied house the next day, grateful for Jenny's offer to watch the baby while she, Elizabeth, tried out the new workshop. The last thing the baby needed was to be exposed to the whine of the band saw and the wood shavings flying off the lathe.

Elizabeth had thought that Travis wasn't the kind of man who'd make a commitment. But what about a proposal of marriage that included accepting responsibility for a child who was not his own? Without stating it in so many words, he'd changed his life-style, relocated. Wasn't all that commitment?

She felt confused by her emotions. There was shock at Travis's proposal, along with her own guilt at reneging on her promise. And although she now knew that keeping Ritchie was her only option, she also knew that her doing it had caused Travis intense heartbreak. She knew instinctively that his bond with the baby was almost as strong as her own. The rending of that bond must be tearing him apart. And she felt a smothering sense of panic as she finally admitted to herself that she was in the position she had fervently hoped to avoid: she was a *single* parent.

She felt alienated. And alone. Again. But now it was a different kind of aloneness. She'd been glad when the divorce had become final; she'd spent far too long having every facet of her personality dissected, weighed and found wanting by Dennis Chapman. But recently, since Travis had come into her life, she'd known that aloneness was only temporary, that he was coming back. Why had she allowed Travis to lull her into a false sense of security?

Because of fear, she realized—fear of committing to him. And deep-seated doubt that he could commit to her. By his own statement, he had never done it before. It had never entered her mind that, in effect, he'd been committed to her from the moment he'd laid eyes on her.

But not now. She'd sent him away. And she knew with awful certainty that he wouldn't be coming back. Now, as she was alone with Ritchie, she realized how solitary her life was. With Brad and Jenny she shared friendship, companionship, and of course, work space. But now, with Travis gone, she had a cavernous empty space within her—an emptiness she hadn't felt since Rick and Kathy had died.

She was reminded of the Frank Capra classic, *It's a Wonderful Life*. It was as if Travis had never existed. If he hadn't, she would have gone through all of this trauma alone. As she was doing now. She blamed *him* for making her care about him.

"You got what you wanted," she told herself morosely. To seal it, she had legal documents from the lawyer couched in language so ice-cold that it made her shiver. Only Travis wasn't there to warm her. . . .

It was only now, as she walked around the unused workshop, that she realized what he'd tried to do. He'd tried to give her the thing she'd always wanted—a sense of belonging to a family. And he'd succeeded in doing that. He'd been just as scared as she, had had no more background than she in having a relationship or raising a child, but he'd forged ahead anyway.

And now she had so much—a child, a home, a place to practice her profession—and he had nothing.

13

As she explored the workshop, Elizabeth almost felt like an intruder, as if she had no right to be there. She went over to the wood storage cabinet, finding everything from black walnut and cherry to such exotics as cocobolo, bubinga, zebrawood. There were even several large burls and sections of seasoned logs, which her fingers itched to turn into free-form bowls and boxes, as well as all kinds of fantastic toys for Ritchie.

After looking at the available stock, she took a log of cherrywood, cutting out a section of it with the band saw. She mounted the roughly trimmed stock on the lathe, then worked it until the natural shape emerged into a paperweight. But even as the wood warmed to her touch, she couldn't entirely forget her surroundings, and the unoccupied house that was a stone's throw away.

Elizabeth's mind took her back to the terrible argument she'd had with Travis after the social worker's visit; he'd described the carriage house as an "empty nest." It had never seemed empty until he'd left. But this house, even with its marvelous workshop, was more than empty: it was barren. She could fill the place to the rafters and it would still be empty, because a vital element would be missing: Travis.

His name had been on the deed. He'd planned to live here. She had the feeling that when she walked through the house, her footsteps echoing in the uninhabited rooms, she would somehow feel Travis's presence beside her.

Her mind was laced with memory pictures of how kind and gentle Travis had been from the first moment he'd seen her, how devotedly he'd cared for her in the early days after Ritchie's birth. He'd stood by her at some of the most devastating times in her life. She remembered his tender declarations of love, declarations she had been unable to respond to.

And all the while he'd been there, he'd asked for nothing except the chance to protect, help, love her. And what had she done for him in return? She'd allowed him occasional access to her body and thrown his marriage proposal back in his face.

She *had* to see him; there was simply no alternative. But what if it was too late, if he turned her away? What if she was too much of a coward to even make the effort? *When are you going to take a risk?* Hadn't she had enough of always being on the outside looking in? she asked herself in disgust, remembering what she'd felt when she'd stood outside the nursery only a while ago.

She finally understood the kind of love he had for her. Not because he had built the magnificent workshop, but because of the immense care that had gone into the planning and execution of it. Would she ever be permitted to plumb the depths of him? Would he let her back into his life after the things she had said and done?

She approached the problem cautiously, as if it were a particularly stubborn burl of wood that was being turned on a lathe for the first time. She would have to be careful. Delicate. A little pressure in the wrong place, and the wood could fly apart into a million jagged pieces....

She left the workshop, taking the paperweight she'd made with her. After picking up Ritchie, she went straight back to the carriage house. But even after getting the baby settled, she couldn't relax. She had the strangest urge to call Travis.

It could only be the result of thinking about him while working in the shop he'd built for her. Finally she called his office and found out that he was at the Palmer House in Chicago for at least the next several days. Her hand shook slightly as she put through the call to his hotel.

"Is Ritchie all right?" he asked immediately, surprised to hear her voice.

"Yes, Ritchie's fine. I'd have told you if he wasn't."

"Then why are you calling?" he asked warily.

The flat tone of his voice scraped across her nerves like nails on a blackboard. "I . . . just wanted to know when you were coming home."

He suppressed the self-pitying impulse to say, *I don't have a home.* The word *home* still had the power to hurt, he found, even half a continent away and connected only by long-distance wire. "Back to Baltimore, you mean? I don't know. I'll let you know when I'd like to see Ritchie." Then, he added, "Snyder told me you'd been to see him."

"Yes, I saw the lawyer. He explained . . . everything. Travis—"

"Look, I'm sorry. I've got a meeting with some people and I've got to get ready for it. Keep me posted on Ritchie."

"Right." Reading between the lines, she had a strong feeling that she wouldn't be seeing him for a long time. Suddenly, she knew that talking to Travis long-distance wasn't enough. If only she could see him face-to-face so he couldn't use the excuse of having to attend a meeting, or having to take an incoming call. According to his itinerary, he was going to be in Chicago for a week; he'd been there four days already. There were three days left before he hit the road again.

After making sure that Jenny didn't mind baby-sitting Ritchie, Elizabeth called a travel agent and arranged for an airline ticket. After packing lightly, she dropped off Ritchie and drove to Baltimore-Washington International Airport. She was in Chicago by dinnertime, at the hotel by early evening. Once there, she went to the front desk and spoke to the registration clerk.

"I'd like Travis Logan's room number, please."

"I'm sorry, but we can't give out that kind of information. We can call upstairs for you, or you can use a house phone."

She chose the latter course, her hand shaking slightly as she picked up the phone.

"What's wrong?" he asked immediately, surprised to hear her voice. "How's Ritchie?"

"Nothing's wrong. He's fine." She took a deep breath. "But I'm not. Can I come up and talk to you?"

"You want to come to *Chicago*?"

To which she replied in a barely steady voice, "I'm here. In the lobby of your hotel. May I come up?"

He shook his head in disbelief. "Room 2732. Take the tower elevator."

The elevator ride seemed to take longer than the plane trip. She was torn between breathless anticipation and a fervent hope that the elevator would be caught between floors. And then there was the endless corridor. She'd barely knocked when the door was opened.

His heart kicked into high gear like a jump-started battery. She looked so wonderful just standing there in the familiar down jacket and beret that it was all he could do to keep from hauling her into his arms by main force. Using all the resources he could command, he fought to control his reactions. "Why are you here, Elizabeth?"

The moment she had dreaded was upon her. Her mind was blank. His voice had been flat and uninterested. And then she got a good look at him and her heart twisted. His mouth was compressed, his eyes dull behind the steel-rimmed glasses, his face unreadable except for lines of fatigue. The striped cotton dress shirt that was tucked into his tan slacks was open at the throat, the cuffs rolled up to his elbows. "I want to come in, Travis."

He stepped aside. She walked toward him, instinctively drawn to the warmth of his body and felt a stab of anguish as he sidestepped sharply, as if he couldn't bear her touch.

"Sit down, Elizabeth."

His manner was perfectly correct. It was also as cold as ice. She had to fight the urge to shiver. Looking around the tastefully decorated hotel room, she saw that she had a choice of two armchairs, a love seat, or the bed. Taking off her jacket and beret, she chose the armchair nearest Travis, who rested his hip on the long dresser set up with his computer equipment.

"What is it you wanted, Elizabeth?"

Another chance, she felt like saying. Aloud, she only told him that she wanted to talk.

"You could just as easily have done that over the phone."

"I don't think so, Travis. You didn't seem terribly anxious to talk the last time I tried."

"All right. The floor's yours. What are you doing here?"

"When you wanted to talk before, I shut you out. I'm sorry. I need—"

Barest nod. "Look, if it's money, or help with the baby—"

"No! I don't need money, or help with Ritchie. You've given me money I didn't want, and the baby's fine. I didn't have to come chasing all over the country for that."

"Then why *did* you come?"

"I . . . I need you, Travis."

"You just discovered that, did you?"

She flinched under the lash of his sarcasm. She wanted to walk away from the pain and embarrassment. But she'd already come so far. She looked up at him. He seemed to be waiting for her to continue.

She wasn't getting anywhere with him, she realized, fighting tears of frustration. Maybe if he could see what she'd created using the workshop he'd given her, he'd be more responsive. She could feel his eyes following her as she walked across the room to her nylon carryon. And as she walked back, carrying the paperweight.

"I made this for you—in the workshop you had Brad build for me." She held it out to him, swallowing hard when he didn't take it. Disappointment thickened her voice as she said, "It's made from a cherrywood log. It doesn't really have any practical use, I guess."

"You're meandering, Elizabeth. Cut to the chase."

"I wanted to thank you for the house."

"Is the workshop equipped to your specifications?"

How excruciatingly polite he was. "Yes. Why did you do it, Travis? Why did you buy the house?"

"So that I could be sure that you and Ritchie would have a home."

"That isn't true."

"Of course it is!" he snapped.

"No, Travis. You bought the house so that the *three* of us could live there. Together. I can't live there by myself."

"*Why?* You signed the papers."

"You threatened me with lawsuits at twenty paces."

"I wouldn't have sued you," he said, his cheekbones tinged with a flush of embarrassment.

"Travis, you accused me of creating an empty nest. Well, this house is no different. It's just as empty."

"It won't be once you live there with Ritchie," he said doggedly.

"I love Ritchie, but he can't fill the empty places. You made me see that I'd created an empty nest for myself at the carriage house. And now you want me to live that way in the house you bought."

"But Ritchie—"

"You said—" she took a deep breath "—you said I should tell you if I needed you."

"I meant it."

"Well, I'm telling you that now, Travis. *I need you.*"

She saw his face pale as he said two devastating words. "For what?"

Trying to frame her response carefully, she said, "I need you in that house you bought for the three of us. I need you, Travis, to be a father to Ritchie, to fill the empty places in the house—in my life and in my heart. I love you, Travis. Unconditionally. With no strings. And I don't say those words lightly."

His heart beating double time, he forced himself to stillness, unwilling, unable to believe that she really meant what she was saying. "I said those same words to you, Elizabeth. Why couldn't you believe that I loved you?" Travis asked.

Loved. He'd used the past tense. She forced herself to go on. "I couldn't prove it."

"It isn't an absolute, like degrees on a thermometer. And how do I believe you now?"

"How do I prove that I love you?" she countered.

"Use any means at your disposal."

"Words aren't enough. You won't believe them."

She saw him turn his head away, and knew that she was losing him. She didn't know how to stop it. And then she saw his hands clasping the edge of the dresser with such force that his knuckles were whitened, his arms stiff, his whole body nearly vibrating under the rigid strictures of control he'd imposed on himself. If she could only break through those barriers.

And then, knowing she was going to be swimming in unfamiliar waters, she got up from the chair and crossed to where he was sitting.

"Leaving, Elizabeth?"

"Not unless you force me out the door." When she got within touching distance, she kissed him lightly on the cheek.

Surprised by her action, he jerked his head away. "What was that for?"

"Words might not mean anything by themselves," she murmured, placing one hand on his stiff shoulder. "I've decided to try another method."

"What . . . method?" he asked, trying to concentrate on controlling his reaction to her nearness.

"Counterpoint."

He stared at her. "What?"

"It's a musical term."

"That much I know."

"In music, it's two themes playing one against the other. Here," she murmured, her voice a mere whisper of air against his ear, "here it means words, in counterpoint with touch." She licked the rim of his ear to emphasize her point. Then she stroked the back of one of his hands, gratified to see his fingers release their death grip on the dresser. She took his hand in hers, tugging gently.

At least he hadn't tried to back away, she noted in relief. And though his eyes were still wary, at least they were no longer the flat, dull color of mud. Maybe her unorthodox method might work, after all. "Come with me."

"Where?"

"Not very far," she assured him.

She led him to the edge of the bed. Then, her hands on either side of his waist, she turned his body until the backs of his legs were at the edge of the mattress. She noticed the rapid pulse in his throat, the slight unevenness in his breathing, the tension in his stance.

She closed the gap between them, anchoring her hands to his shoulders, and using the front of his body for leverage. Linking her hands behind his neck, she urged his head downward so that her mouth was within striking distance of his. It was hard to pull away.

As her lips rubbed back and forth against his, her fingers slowly released the buttons of his shirt. One . . . by . . . one. As each button was released, her fingers slowly parted the fabric, her mouth explored the exposed skin of his chest.

As her fingers reached his waist, she drew the fabric from his slacks, undoing the last button before easing the shirt off his shoulders, down his arms, and allowing it to fall to the floor. She felt him sway, then wondered how long she herself could withstand the wave of heat that washed over her.

Her eyes dropped to his waist, and to the belt buckle that bisected it. Her fingers hovered over the buckle, barely touching it. *I can't do this,* she groaned inwardly, feeling her face flame. *Yes, you can,* an inner voice taunted.

"Need any help?" Travis asked.

"No, thank you." She managed to unclasp the buckle, and the hook at his waist. Her breath caught in her throat when her trembling hands encountered the surge of pulsating heat that was barely restrained by taut fabric. She carefully unzipped the slacks and eased them—and his briefs—away from his hips. She licked her lips; she felt damp all over, her breath was coming in short, uneven puffs, her mouth was dry.

Then Travis sat down on the edge of the bed and removed his shoes and socks, utterly bemused at what she was trying to do, captivated and in love all over again.

Yielding to the light pressure of her hands on his shoulders, he lay back on the bed, never taking his eyes from hers. Lying naked while she was fully clothed, he felt oddly vulnerable. Moments later, however, clothing was no longer an issue, as she quickly removed her own clothes and lay on the bed beside him.

She closed her eyes in an attempt to gather her thoughts together. "I know now that there's a bond between us that can't be broken. I know how strong it is, because I tried to break it and failed." As she spoke, Elizabeth removed Travis's steel-rimmed glasses, then placed soft kisses on his closed eyes. "You gave and gave. With caring, tenderness, humor, and no thought of self." She tunneled her fingers into his hair, gently anchoring him to the pillow.

"Don't make me out a saint, Elizabeth," he said thickly.

"How do I love you, Travis?" she asked, cupping his face between her two hands. "Let me count the ways." Her mouth pressed a moist kiss to his. "I love you for your passion, and gentleness, and because you're the sexiest thing that ever happened to me. But I also love you because you turned your life and life-style upside down and inside out for a child whose existence you could never have suspected, and a woman you'd never heard of, never even met." Her tongue probed the depths of his mouth, and she felt she was losing herself in the process.

"You gave until there was nothing left for you. You gave me a family, while you have none for yourself. You gave me the house, and the workshop, while you have an anonymous hotel room in another city on the road. I have Ritchie. I can survive. Thanks to you, I can survive very well. But I'm not complete. Not without you. You've given me so much, Travis. Are you always going to give me everything I want?" she asked, her mouth lapping at the salty moisture that had pooled at the hollow of his throat.

"What is it . . . you want?" he gasped, his senses heightened to fever pitch at the growing tightness in his groin.

She concentrated on suckling his nipples, each one in turn, coaxing them into erectness. And loving the way his body shifted in response. "A second chance. A new beginning. You." She laid her cheek against his chest, her mouth pressing a kiss to the region of his heart. "I'm tired of empty nests and substitute loves. I can't live in that house without you. The place is so empty. I can't fill it alone."

One hand stroked the familiar shock of damp hair from his forehead, the other hand descending to his tautly muscled stomach. "Woodworkers pay special attention to texture, grain, hardness." She felt his indrawn breath as her insistent hand descended lower. "When I'm working with a piece of wood, I have to use a delicate touch to find perfection. The perfect form," she whispered. "I can hold that piece of wood in my hand. Like this—" her fingers closing gently around his pulsating masculine heat "—and sand it. And shape it. Until it's smooth. Like this. And so very warm—" her knowing fingers applying loving friction "—like this."

He arched against her, her sensual exploration arousing him almost past the point of no return.

Bracing her hands lightly on his rib cage for support, she straddled his hips, poising herself above him. "I remember when you said that I wasn't the only one that wanted to be part of a family, that you wanted it as much as I did. That you wanted a place to call home. I hope you still want that. No more empty spaces," she whispered, her hand trembling as she guided him to the brink of her moist warmth.

"No...more," he groaned, his fingers biting into her waist as his body took over the seduction she had begun. Unable to hold back any longer, he arched upward, sheathing himself to the hilt, plunging both of them into a shattering climax of passion.

SHE RETURNED to awareness slowly. Her cheek was resting just under his chin, her breath soughing gently against his damp skin. Her full breasts were crushed against his chest. And he was still filling the emptiness within her the most intimate way possible, maintaining the bond that couldn't be broken.

"Did I convince you?" She paused for but a second. "Do you believe that I love you?"

Hugging her close to him, Travis looked up into turquoise eyes that were glazed, filled to overflowing.

"Yes, I believe you," he murmured, shifting to his side and taking her with him. "What am I going to do with you, Elizabeth?"

She cuddled close to him. "Love me."

"That's a given, honey. I love you. And I can't live without you," he said, inexpressibly moved by each gesture, each touch, each kiss that had been steeped in tenderness. "I just don't seem to be able to help myself, Elizabeth. Anything else?"

"Yes. Two things," she breathed, barely able to control the empassioned tremors that threatened to overwhelm her.

"What, honey?"

She poured all the tenderness she was capable of into the deeply yearning kiss that threatened to reignite the sensual fires that had recently burned between them. "Marry me, Travis," she implored softly, "and take me home."

Back by Popular Demand

Janet Dailey
Americana

A romantic tour of America through fifty favorite Harlequin Presents, each set in a different state researched by Janet and her husband, Bill. A journey of a lifetime in one cherished collection.

In July, don't miss the exciting states featured in:

Title #11 — HAWAII
     Kona Winds

#12 — IDAHO
     The Travelling Kind

Available wherever
Harlequin books are sold.

 **Harlequin Books®**

GREAT NEWS...

HARLEQUIN UNVEILS NEW SHIPPING PLANS

For the convenience of customers, Harlequin has announced that Harlequin romances will now be available in stores at these convenient times each month*:

Harlequin Presents, American Romance, Historical, Intrigue:

> May titles: April 10
> June titles: May 8
> July titles: June 5
> August titles: July 10

Harlequin Romance, Superromance, Temptation, Regency Romance:

> May titles: April 24
> June titles: May 22
> July titles: June 19
> August titles: July 24

We hope this new schedule is convenient for you.

With only two trips each month to your local bookseller, you'll never miss any of your favorite authors!

*Please note: There may be slight variations in on-sale dates in your area due to differences in shipping and handling.

HDATES-RR

*Applicable to U.S. only.

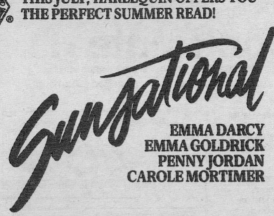